W9-BSO-535

MARV

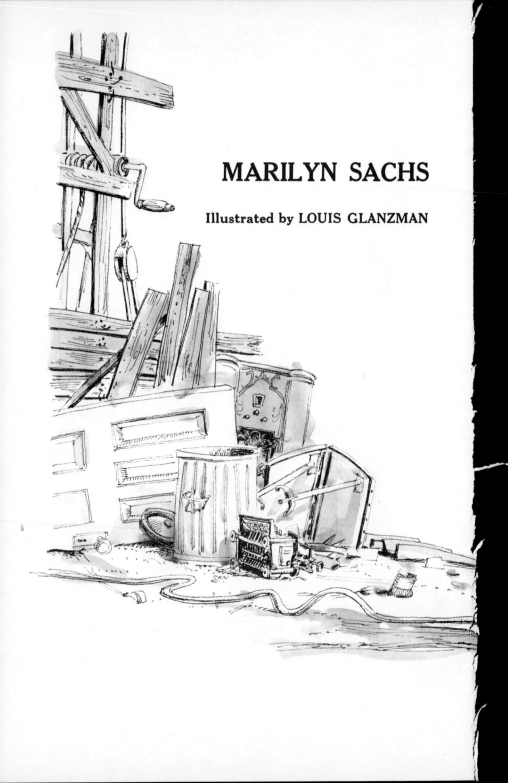

MARILYN SACHS

Illustrated by LOUIS GLANZMAN

MARV

DOUBLEDAY & COMPANY, INC.

GARDEN CITY, NEW YORK

1970

By Marilyn Sachs

Amy Moves In
Laura's Luck
Amy and Laura
Veronica Ganz
Peter and Veronica
Marv

LIBRARY OF CONGRESS CATALOG CARD NUMBER 73–116250

COPYRIGHT © 1970 BY MARILYN SACHS

PRINTED IN THE UNITED STATES OF AMERICA

FIRST EDITION

For Mimi and Alice. And for Morris—
who knows Marv Green better than anyone else.

1

"Marv! *Marv!*"

Marv Green grabbed a paper bag from the top of the refrigerator. It still had a few oranges in it. But he could hear her footsteps approaching down the hall. Quickly he scooped all the wires and springs spread out on the kitchen table into the bag, plus the shell of the old clock. Then he dropped the bag under the table, and had a moment or two to wonder why he hadn't just left everything as it was before Frances opened the door.

"Hello, Frances," he said, feeling guilty.

"Where's Mama?"

7

Marv poked the bag with his toe, and looked at his sister's red, red cheeks. They weren't red from the weather. Her eyes were narrowed, her mouth was tight, and she was angry. Not at him though. That was good. She wanted Mama this time.

"Uh—I don't know. I just got home myself an hour ago, and I've been busy since."

"Doing what?" Frances' eyes swept the empty kitchen table.

"This and that . . ." Quickly he asked, "What do you want Mama for?"

There was a thump from the outside door, and the slow, heavy sound of footsteps under a heavy load. Queenie, who never bothered for anybody else, began barking. She came out from her warm spot under the stove, and whined at the kitchen door.

"There's Mama," said Frances, and she hurried out of the room. Marv heard her say, "Why do you carry all that yourself? Here, give me one. Why don't you ask somebody to help you? Why . . . ?"

Why was he hiding that bag under the table, Marv wondered. He bent down, picked it up, and thought, I've got nothing to be ashamed of. So what if she does see it?

"Why . . ." Frances' voice, nearer this time, "don't you just ask? What's the matter with you that you can't ask Marv? What's he doing that's so important that he can't help his mother carry bundles that are too heavy for her? Why . . . ?"

They were right outside the door now. Marv yanked open the refrigerator door, jammed the bag in as far as he could, slammed the door, and rushed forward to help his mother.

She was carrying a bulky, brown paper bag. Behind her came Frances with an equally bulky bag.

"Here, Mama, give it to me," said Marv, holding out his arms.

"No, no, I'm fine," his mother protested.

Then, the bottom of her bag just seemed to give way, and oranges, grapefruits, lemons and a large jar of sour pickles tumbled down over her legs and onto the floor. Mrs. Green moaned suddenly, sat down on a kitchen chair, and burst into tears.

"All day," she said, "it's been like this. All day. Not just one thing, but everything. *Everything*. All day!"

She buried her face in her hands, and wept in loud, intense sobs. Queenie, after sniffing bleakly at everything on the floor, joined in with a wheezy whine.

"Don't cry, Mama," Marv said. "I'll pick everything up. It's all right." He knelt down on the floor, and quickly began gathering up oranges and grapefruits. "Look, the jar of pickles didn't even break. Just a little pickle juice got out. Don't cry, Mama. We can still eat the pickles."

"It's not," Frances said savagely, standing by the door, "the pickles that are making her cry."

Their mother's sobs increased in volume. Helplessly, Marv sat down on the floor and watched her. He knew that about once a year or so, his mother was visited with an "attack of nerves" as she described it. The rest of the time she never cried, seldom raised her voice, and generally seemed able to endure each day's problems with good-natured resignation. Nobody knew what made it happen or why one particular day of troubles was harder to bear than another. Without warning, she would start to cry—hard and loud and long. It could last anywhere from twenty minutes to an hour. When it was over, no side effects remained, and another year might pass before the same thing happened all over again.

So it was with a familiar sort of sympathy that Marv watched her from his seat on the floor. He hated to see her cry, but he also knew it would pass.

"I know," said Frances once more, "that it has nothing to do with the pickles."

"Pickles, schmickles," came his mother's voice from underneath the sobs. "That should be my worst troubles—pickles!"

But Frances' cheeks were still flaming. She narrowed her eyes and tightened her mouth even more as she looked toward her mother. Whatever it was that was bothering Frances, now was not the time to be worrying their mother with it. At the risk of turning her attention upon himself, Marv urged softly, "Leave her alone, Frances. She'll be all right. Why don't you help me pick up the grapefruits."

"You!" Frances hissed. "You! Some great son you

are! Just look at you. Anybody can insult your mother, and what do you do?" She waved her free hand at him. The other one was still holding the package. "What do you do? . . . Sit in the grapefruits!"

Mrs. Green moaned. "All day! First the toilet overflowed, and I ran down to the basement to get the plunger. So I locked myself out, and I had to bang on the door, and wake Papa up. That's bad enough, but by the time he heard me, and by the time I got it fixed, I forgot all about my honey cake in the oven. All right, so it burned. What can you do? That's life. So then, here's a letter from my brother in Buffalo. His Alvin, you know, the youngest one, was rushed to the hospital, so sick he nearly died. Why such a young boy should have something wrong like that, something ruptured in his appendix—why it should happen to him, such a nice, quiet boy! But—thank God, it's over with. He'll get better but he has to stay in the hospital another couple of weeks. So then I go out shopping, and . . ."

"Yes," said Frances between clenched teeth, "and Mr. Zelitsky insulted you. I know all about it. Mrs. Tannenbaum stopped me as I was coming home, and said she was in the store, and if it was her, she would have fallen through the floor."

"All I said," sobbed Mrs. Green, her tears bouncing off the table, "was please Mr. Zelitsky, make sure it's fresh, and maybe trim a little of the fat before you weigh it, please."

11

"Why don't you go to another butcher?" Marv suggested.

It was not the first time that he or some other member of the family had made such a suggestion. Mr. Zelitsky, the butcher, had a reputation for not only having the best kosher meat anywhere in the Bronx, but the meanest disposition as well. Not one of his customers liked him. "For every lamb chop a customer buys, Mr. Zelitsky gives away free an insult," Marv's mother had said many times.

Frances snorted, and his mother continued sobbing.

"Papa says you should find another butcher," Marv continued. "He says nobody should buy from a maniac like Zelitsky."

"Papa!" Frances said disdainfully.

Marv shook his head, but he didn't say anything. He wasn't going to start up again with Frances. Once a day was enough to start up with Frances. Nobody in the Green family was a match for her. But up until this past fall, when she became seventeen, and started going to Hunter College, at least Papa was safe. Before that, for as long as Marv could remember, Frances had brow-beaten, badgered, criticized, instructed, and consistently found fault with himself, his fifteen-year-old sister Betsy, and Mama. Papa, up until September of 1939, had not been a target. But now he was.

According to Frances, Papa and his generation were responsible for the war that was raging on in Europe and Asia right now. They were responsible for the rise of fascism, for Hitler, Mussolini, Hirohito, and Franco. Why, Frances demanded to know, hadn't Papa and his generation made sure after the First World War that it all wouldn't have to happen again. Why had they been so blind? All over the world now people were dying—because of Papa, and people like him.

Her disapproval of Papa was not only confined to his politics. She had serious reservations about his union activities, and grave doubts about his attitude toward his family. He was, in Frances' eyes, overindulgent as a father (in regard to Betsy and Marv) and negligent as a husband.

"How can Papa allow anybody to talk to his wife like that?" cried Frances.

"But she doesn't have to buy there," Marv protested weakly. "She could buy from another butcher who isn't so mean."

"Nobody," their mother wept, "has such meat as that louse, Zelitsky."

"And then, there's a principle involved here," said Frances. "Mama has the right to shop wherever she pleases, and should be treated with dignity anywhere she chooses to go. Why should this Zelitsky feel free to insult her? Does he talk to his rich customers the way he talks to her? Are his rich customers any better than your mother?

"And another thing," Frances continued, her eyes flashing, "if you were half a man, and you're thirteen years old—you're not a baby any more—you wouldn't be sitting there letting your mother be insulted by everybody."

"It was just Mr. Zelitsky, not everybody, and I don't even know what he said."

". . . a piece of flank steak," sobbed their mother. "It looked a little black, so I just said, like in a joke, 'Didn't I see that same piece of meat lying there last week?' He had to call me a liar?"

"There," snapped Frances, "a liar. He called your mother a liar. But that's all right. She's only a woman, after all, and as far as you and Papa are concerned, a woman's honor doesn't really count. Sure, Papa can go on sleeping like nothing's happened, and you—you might as well put some finishing touches on that new monstrosity you've got in the garden. As usual, when somebody has to protect Mama, I'm the only one around."

In his brain, the drums started beating. *Bong*, bong, bong, bong, *bong*, bong, bong, bong. Sooner or later, whenever Frances went to work on him, that beating started in his head. He could feel the hot flash roaring through his brain, and singeing the hairs on his neck. His fingers began to curl, and his knees to jerk. There was no stopping it once it started.

"You're right, you're right!" he shouted, jumping up. "He called my mother a liar. Why should he call my mother a liar? He's got no right to call my mother a liar."

"But he did call your mother a liar. He called your

14

mother a liar," Frances practically chanted. "And last week, he called her a pest, and the week before he said she should get out of his store. Do you think he says that to his rich customers?"

". . . no place to go," sobbed Mrs. Green. "That meat the butcher on 168th Street has is like straw, and the one on Boston Road is even worse. I think he colors his meat. Oiy—such a day, and later I lost my glove, and . . ."

"What should I do, Frances? Tell me what to do."

"Make sure it never happens again." Frances pulled Marv toward her. "It's a matter of simple justice. Your mother is weak and defenseless, and this man is a bully. Let him know she's not as defenseless as he thinks. Let him see that there's one man in the Green family who won't stand by and see her insulted." She gave him a little push toward the door.

Bong, bong, bong, bong, *bong*, bong, bong, bong.

"I'm going," Marv cried, and tore out of the kitchen.

"Marvin!" came his mother's voice after him, "Marvin!"

But he knew better than to turn back now. Once he turned back, he might never get started again. And he had a score to settle, and it had better be settled fast before the rhythmic throbbing in his head died away. Beware Zelitsky, the Butcher. A champion comes.

2

Marv was halfway down the street when he realized that he wasn't wearing a jacket. For a moment the thought of going back and getting one did make him slow down. But what kind of a person are you, and what kind of a person would Frances think you are, and let you know too, if you could even think about jackets when your mother has been called a liar.

Hurtling down the street, Marv refused to let his attention wander from the matter at hand. Those two empty orange crates in front of Dubin's Grocery would no doubt still be there on his return, and why should anybody call his mother a liar. Mr. Robinson, the super of the corner apartment house should watch where he was sweeping, and boy, would he tell Mr. Zelitsky that nobody, but nobody, can call Marv Green's mother a liar and get away with it.

"Excuse me, Mrs. Rose, I didn't see you. I'm sorry. I'm sorry. I *said* I was sorry."

Bong, bong, bong, bong. He had to run fast to keep the drums going. Already they sounded a little far off. A half a block now, only a half a block onward, and Mr. Zelitsky would never forget how to talk to a lady, particularly if she was Marv Green's mother.

Through the window, between the chickens and one duck, hanging from hooks, Marv could see Mr. Zelitsky all alone in the store. He flung open the door, and rushed in, the wind behind him blowing up the sawdust that lay sprinkled all over the floor.

The butcher was sawing away on a huge hunk of meat that lay on his block. He was a short, heavy man with broad shoulders. His eyebrows met across the top of his nose, and there were dark patches of hair on each of his fingers. He was talking to himself as he worked. The words were not clear but the meaning was, and even as Marv approached he could hear the vehemence that lay behind the butcher's words. It sounded like *vit—vat—veet*. On each *veet*, Mr. Zelitsky seemed to lean on the saw with all his might, and give it a particularly murderous thrust.

BONG, bong.

18

"Mr. Zelitsky!" Marv thundered in a cracked whisper.

"*Vit—vat—veet—veet.*" Mr. Zelitsky gave two vicious swoops with the saw, and looked up at Marv.

"What? What? What do you want, boy? Marvin? What do you want?"

Bong.

Marv said fast. "You called my mother a liar, Mr. Zelitsky, and I don't think that's right because my mother's no liar, and I don't want anybody to .call· her a liar anyway because she's my mother, and you have no right to call my mother even if she is your customer a liar because she's my mother too, Mr. Zelitsky, so don't call her a liar . . ."

"A liar," screamed Mr. Zelitsky, looking straight over Marv's shoulder, "that's just what *he* is—a liar."

The beating was completely gone from Marv's head. So was the fire. He felt cold, and a little embarrassed that he'd gone and made that long speech, and Mr. Zelitsky hadn't even been listening.

"Please Mr. Zelitsky," Marv urged, "listen to me for just one minute. I want to ask you—please—not to call my mother a liar . . ."

Mr. Zelitsky leaned on the saw, and pulled it back and forth through the meat. "Liar," cried Mr. Zelitsky in the direction of the blade. "Not even three months, and you told me at least a year. You crook, Sherman, you liar. You didn't even fix it."

Marv moved in a little closer, and watched the way the blade of the saw wobbled.

"Liar!" repeated Mr. Zelitsky, and lapsed into his own private conversation again. *"Vit—vat—veet."*

"You know," said Marv, his eyes tracing the wobbling blade to the wobbling wing nut that held the blade bolt to the body of the saw, "I think I know what's wrong. Just let me have a look, Mr. Zelitsky."

"Three dollars and eighty-eight cents," said the butcher fiercely, "for a new blade, and it's no better than the old one."

"Let me have a look," Marv repeated.

"Look, look. As long as it doesn't cost me anything." He held out the saw, and Marv took it, and tenderly turned the wing nut. It was impossible to tighten. The malady was apparent.

"You have a stripped thread on your blade bolt," Marv said briskly. "That's why the blade isn't cutting properly."

"Three dollars and eighty-eight cents," said Mr. Zelitsky, his black eyes nearly starting out of his head, "and I think it's even worse than the old blade."

"It has nothing to do with the blade," Marv explained patiently. "Because the thread is stripped, the wing nut isn't holding, and that's why the blade wobbles."

"You mean nothing's wrong with the blade?"

"Nothing, Mr. Zelitsky." Marv ran a practiced finger lightly over the teeth of the blade. "Everything seems fine. All you need to do is put in a washer here in front of the nut, and your saw will be as good as new."

He smiled encouragingly at the saw, gave it a friendly pat, and held it out to the butcher.

"But I just bought a new blade," said Mr. Zelitsky stubbornly, "for three eighty-eight. That crook who sharpens my knives and fixes them, that Sherman, put it in for me, and he swore I wouldn't have any trouble with it."

"And you won't," Marv said kindly. "All you need is a washer."

"Washer? Like for a sink?"

"Not that kind. The little metal kind. You must have some. Everybody has washers."

"I don't know." Mr. Zelitsky pulled out a drawer from a table behind him, and looked helplessly at its collection of pencils, Coca-Cola bottle tops, screws, nails, rubber bands, and other assorted articles. "Come here, Marvin. Maybe you'll see it."

Marv came around the counter, and looked in the drawer. He poked aside a few clips, and looked under several beer openers. There was a whole pile of washers under the beer openers.

"Here's one," said Marv, holding a washer out to the butcher. "Just slip this on in front of the wing nut."

"What wing nut?" moaned the butcher. "Who knows from wing nuts. For three eighty-eight you'd think that Sherman would have thrown in a good wink knot, or whatever it is."

The door opened. Again the sawdust scattered, and in came a customer.

"What do *you* want?" yelled Mr. Zelitsky at her, as if the last thing he wanted to see in his store were customers.

"Please Mr. Zelitsky," said the woman apologetically, "do you have some nice veal cutlets?"

"Of course I have nice veal cutlets. What do you think—I don't have nice veal cutlets?"

"I know you have nice veal cutlets," replied the lady soothingly, smiling a timid smile, "and if you don't mind, could you let me have three please."

"My customers should only be as nice as my veal cutlets," retorted Mr. Zelitsky. He turned to look at Marv. "Now tell me, Marvin, this is a big job that has to be done on the saw?"

"No, Mr. Zelitsky, it'll only take a few minutes. All you have to do is . . ."

"Look, Marvin, be a good boy, and do it for me, all right? I have to take care of her." A furious shrug of his shoulders, and Mr. Zelitsky advanced on his customer.

Most of the meat in Mr. Zelitsky's store, as in other kosher butcher stores, was kept in a huge, walk-in refrigerator at the back of the store. Each time a customer asked for a particular cut of meat, the butcher had to walk to the refrigerator, open the heavy door, take down the meat from a hook inside, carry it out to the cutting block, slice off the requested piece, and either carry what remained back to the refrigerator right away or hang it up on one of a number of hooks attached to the wall.

Nothing was pre-cut. A Jewish matron might tolerate delay, higher prices and even bad temper on the part of the butcher, but she would only buy her meat custom tailored to her specifications.

"Three veal cutlets from the shoulder, and about this thick, Mr. Zelitsky. And then a piece of calves' liver for my boy. He's sick, so I don't want it too dark, and no strings. Then maybe I'll take one baby rib chop for my Tessie's baby—a little one, Mr. Zelitsky, and it has to be very tender because the baby doesn't have any teeth yet, God bless her . . ."

Back and forth the butcher trudged. Marv had the washer in place, and was just proceeding to put the wing nut back where it belonged when Mr. Zelitsky staggered by, on his way back to the refrigerator. He had a huge piece of liver in his arms, and was muttering fiercely. Two other customers had arrived, and were awaiting their turn. The liver in Mr. Zelitsky's arms was jiggling so hard he had trouble keeping it from bouncing away.

"Here—you—Marvin—open this door for me. Hurry!"

Marv laid down the saw, grabbed the heavy handle of the door, and finally managed to open it. He watched the butcher stagger into the refrigerator, hang up the liver on one hook, remove a piece of lamb from another, stagger out of the refrigerator, and by thrusting his body against the door, manage to close it.

An electric eye, Marv thought immediately. He needs an electric eye. He walked back to the table, picked up the saw but couldn't keep his eyes off the butcher. He watched as Mr. Zelitsky flung the meat down on the cutting block, sliced off the piece required by his customer, and this time, hung the remaining meat on a hook against the wall.

An electric eye, Marv thought. So then, if he's carrying something, he won't need a free hand to open the door. He laid the saw down, leaned against the table, and looked thoughtfully at the piece of meat hanging from the hook. Right next to it was another hook with another piece of meat hanging from it. And next to that was another hook with some hot dogs draped over it. Sometime during the course of the day, Mr. Zelitsky would have to remove all that meat from the hooks, carry it to the refrigerator, and hang it up on hooks inside. He would also have to open the door each time.

"It's too fatty?" Mr. Zelitsky was shouting at his current victim. "You should only look so thin as this piece of meat."

Sure he's mean and nasty, Marv thought, sitting down on the table. He's tired from all that lifting and carrying and walking. But if he had an electric eye installed in front of his refrigerator, he wouldn't have to work so hard. Marv concentrated on the hooks. Wasn't there something else? Something he was missing? Of course. Why not have those hooks run along a track instead of being fixed to the wall? If that was the case, Mr. Zelitsky wouldn't even have to carry the meat back to the refrigerator. All he'd have to do was simply press a lever with his foot—it could be under the block—and the track would move the meat back to the refrigerator door. It would be waiting there for him to come and take it down. No! Marv nearly laughed out loud. He wouldn't even need to take it down. He would only have to approach the door, activate the electric eye, and when the door opened, step on another lever inside. That would move the meat into the refrigerator, and then he could take it down, and put it on the other hooks.

Marv hit his head. What a dope he was! Another lever inside the refrigerator could control a moving, pincer-like part that would remove the meat from the one hook and return it to the other.

And why stop there? You don't cure pneumonia just by treating the patient's leg. Marv looked around the small untidy butcher store. He looked at the growling, untidy butcher. A butcher store rose up in his mind like what a butcher store ought to be.

Every door in the store was opened by electric eyes. Two tracks ran down the ceiling—one carrying the meat to the refrigerator, and one carrying it from. A series of levers, painted different colors were placed on the floor behind the butcher's block. By pressing the red one, a piece of beef was brought out from the refrigerator. Pressing it a second time returned the meat to the refrigerator. Blue brought the veal, and yellow the lamb.

Not only the meat but the customers as well could be maneuvered in and out of the store by means of movable chairs. They could enjoy canned music while they waited their turns, and feast their eyes on colorful paintings of famous butchers or famous animals or maybe just flowers.

And standing behind the butcher's block, resplendent in a clean, white suit—no—*sitting* behind the butcher's block, resplendent in a clean, white suit was Mr. Zelitsky, smiling. That's right, smiling. No longer overworked, he could talk pleasantly to his customers, and smile at them, while the quality of his meat remained unchanged.

He smiled at the butcher. Mr. Zelitsky was standing right next to him. Mr. Zelitsky was not smiling. Mr. Zelitsky was speaking. Mr. Zelitsky was not speaking. Mr. Zelitsky was yelling, "*Why are you sitting on my saw?*"

It took only a moment for Marv to be transported back to the small, untidy store. Quickly he stood up, took the saw, and began tightening the wing nut as Mr. Zelitsky turned to glower at his next cutomer.

There. It was done. The wing nut grasped the thread securely. The blade held taut. Marv raised it in his hand, and swiped the air with it. Once more to make sure . . .

"Marv!"

Such a horrible, terrifying shriek! Through the door raced Frances. Everything froze. The lady reaching over the counter for her meat, Mr. Zelitsky holding out his hand for money, and right behind him, Marv, with saw raised high above the butcher's head.

Frances kept screaming, "Put it down . . . put it down . . . I didn't mean you should *kill* him ... . come right home . . . don't worry about anything else . . . just come . . . right now . . . hurry . . . put it down!"

So he put the saw down, came around the counter, allowed Frances to grab his arm, both arms as a matter of fact, and hurry him to the door. He couldn't help seeing her face. It was terror-stricken, a look he had never seen on it before.

"Marvin," Mr. Zelitsky called out just before they reached the door. He should have just continued going, on out the door. Maybe if he had, Frances might have gone on thinking of him as a potential murderer, and not been upset by learning the truth. But he stopped, even though Frances kept tugging at him, looked back, and there was the butcher jabbing the air with the saw. "Marvin," he said tenderly, "let me give you something—a pound of chop meat, a few hot dogs . . ."

"That's all right, Mr. Zelitsky," Frances cried, and

there was a note of pride in her voice. "You don't have to give my brother anything. He doesn't want anything from you."

"So all right," said Mr. Zelitsky, and he smiled. It was the first time Marv had seen him smile. "Let me at least say thank you. Marvin, you're smarter than I thought." He sliced the air with the saw. "Look how it works—better than new. You're some fixer, boychik!"

"Some fixer!" said Frances bitterly as they walked along home. She wasn't holding his arm any more. In fact, she was a foot or two out in front while he tried to maintain a discreet distance behind her.

But she turned, and there was the familiar Frances face again—disdainful and angry.

"Fixer, my foot," she said. "You're a failure, that's what you are. A failure!"

3

"Failure" was a word Marv was familiar with. He
had heard it on Frances' lips for as long as he could
remember. Its echoes had reverberated back to him out
of the mouths of just about all of his regular teachers
with the exception of Mrs. Chandler, his kindergarten
teacher, and Miss Jackson, the substitute teacher in
fifth grade. Mrs. Chandler had been too busy putting
on galoshes, wiping weepy eyes and noses, and teaching everybody to stand in line to have any time left
over to think about failure. However, Miss Jackson,
who was the substitute teacher during the six weeks
that Mrs. Roper was in the hospital with a broken hip,

had not considered him a failure. Miss Jackson even liked him. It was the first time in his entire school career that a teacher had singled him out for liking.

Of course, Miss Jackson was only a substitute teacher. She was so pretty, she didn't even look like a teacher, and she wore perfume so she didn't even smell like one. But she had liked him. For one thing, she never tore up his drawings when she caught him doodling. All the other teachers did. And they were right, weren't they? He knew very well that he'd never learn anything doodling when he was supposed to be doing something useful. You couldn't blame a teacher for getting sore. It wasn't as if he had any talent. He knew that without them telling him.

But Miss Jackson never took away his drawings. A couple of times he was even surprised and shocked that she did not. That one time, for instance, when they were supposed to be working on Roman numerals, she'd passed right by his desk, and he knew she saw that drawing of the sun dial for cloudy days.

Maybe she thought because he had Roman numerals on the dial, he was doing the assignment in a way. But then there was the time the class was supposed to be writing a composition about *A Haunted House.* She had stood right up near his desk for a few minutes before he knew she was there, watching him draw the skeleton key that turns on the lights the same time it opens the door.

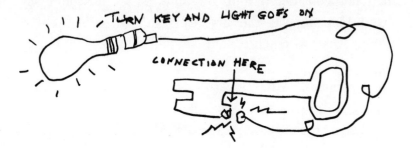

You couldn't really say that had a thing to do with haunted houses.

And then she was forever asking him to empty the waste paper baskets and to fill the inkwells, a sure sign that a teacher likes you. So he was very sorry when Miss Jackson told the class one Friday afternoon that Mrs. Roper's hip had healed, and that she would be coming back to teach them on Monday. Miss Jackson said she wanted to say goodbye. She said she had enjoyed teaching them, and that she would miss them all very much. It seemed to Marv that she was looking at him when she said it, so he dragged his feet a little that afternoon, and hung around after everybody else in the class left.

He just wanted to say goodbye, and maybe apologize for not always paying attention. To his amazement, before he even opened his mouth, she asked if he would be willing to give her the drawing he'd made that afternoon while the class was supposed to be reading an Indian legend. He hadn't even thought she'd seen him at it. And why she'd want it he couldn't imagine, unless she was planning to show it to the principal.

So reluctantly, he pulled it out of his book. It was a drawing of a mechanical blanket attached to a swivel that could be used for sending Indian smoke signals without the sender standing over a fire and getting smoke in his eyes. There was a grease stain up in the left hand corner from that part of his whitefish sandwich that had remained on his thumb. She smiled when she looked at it so he knew she wasn't going to show it to the principal. She stood up, put an arm across his shoulder and walked with him to the door. He could smell her perfume, and was suddenly so embarrassed that he couldn't even look up. So maybe he didn't hear it right, but it seemed to him that she said, "I'm so happy to have your wonderful drawing, Marv. I'll have it framed, and hang it up in my living room."

No, he must have heard her wrong, and he certainly could not blame Mrs. Roper or any real teacher for getting irritated at his doodling. Maybe he was just plain "stupid" the way Mrs. Edgars, the sixth-grade teacher said. The only subject he was really good in was shop, but then stupid kids were supposed to be good in shop. He had been in the 2 class since third grade, and what with being left back in Mrs. Edgar's class, you couldn't wonder that Frances considered him a failure.

From the relatively safe distance of half a block, he

watched Frances flounce up the stairs of their house, and swing the door closed behind her. Except for Marv's house and the one next to it, every house on the street was an apartment house. Some were red brick. Some were yellow. Some were gray. All were over four stories high.

Only Marv's house and its neighbor were one family houses. Each had a tiny green patch of ground, a line of privet hedge, and a row of wooden steps leading up to the door. The houses were attached, and seemed to huddle against each other for protection against their giant neighbors.

He counted up to 178 after Frances disappeared before he approached the house. He could hear his mother humming *The Blue Danube Waltz* as he walked through the hall, and when he cautiously stuck his head through the kitchen door, he was relieved to see that, aside from Queenie under the stove, she was the only one in the room.

"Uh, Mama—where's Frances?"

His mother was frying something that smelled delicious. He hoped it was potato latkes. She looked at him with a friendly, untroubled face. "I think she's inside," and then added with a smile, "You're hungry, Marvin? Come, have a latke."

Holding the crisp, sizzling potato pancake on a fork, and blowing at it, Marv could see that all was back to normal again in regard to his mother. Funny how he didn't feel at all guilty about having failed her as he certainly had. She seemed to have forgotten all her troubles as she watched her son eat the latke. When he was through, she nodded before he even asked, took the fork from him, and speared another spluttering latke from out of the pan.

The alarm clock went off from the big bedroom. "Six o'clock already," said Mrs. Green, "Papa's getting up."

Marvin's father was a bread baker. He worked all night, and slept all day. His family saw him at supper-time, and sometimes, if he didn't stop off at the Union, at breakfast. He didn't have to go to work until after they were asleep, but usually his evenings were filled with union affairs. He was secretary of Bakers Union, Local 27.

Just as Papa emerged from his bedroom, Frances burst back into the kitchen. Her eyes skimmed over her father, rested with disgust for a moment on Marv, and focused finally on her mother.

"Mama, I have to be out of here by 6:30. When are we eating?"

"Right away," said Mrs. Green. "I'll just cook a few onions, and cut up some vegetables . . ."

"Oh, Mama, I don't have the time to wait. If I don't get over to the library by seven, I'll never finish my work."

"What are you working on, Frances?" asked her father pleasantly.

"On the nature of carbon compounds," Frances said

unpleasantly. "I doubt if you'd be interested. Mama, if supper isn't on the table in fifteen minutes I'm not eating." She stamped out of the room, and Mr. Green sighed and said, "What happened today?"

"I don't know." Mrs. Green looked at Marv. "You didn't upset her, did you, Marvin?" she asked in a lowered voice. The three of them moved closer together.

"I always upset her," Marv said sadly. "I can't help myself."

His mother made a deep, mournful noise in her throat. "She's such a high strung girl, you shouldn't say anything to upset her."

"I try, Mama, but anything I say upsets her."

They were whispering now. Mrs. Green looked uneasily over her shoulder in the direction of the bedroom that Frances shared with Betsy.

"She's such a brilliant girl. Her teachers, everybody says so," said Mr. Green. "I guess she'd be better off with a more intelligent, educated family. There's nobody she can talk to."

"Don't blame yourself, Irving," said his wife. "You do the best you can for her. I think maybe it's my fault. When she was a baby and she had the colic I didn't like how the doctor took away the milk from her. You remember I told him but maybe I should have given it to her anyway. I don't think she had enough nourishment when she was a baby. That's why she's so high strung now."

Their heads were practically touching when Betsy opened the kitchen door and came into the room. They had been so absorbed in their conversation that they hadn't heard her approach. She had a very light step as it was—light and graceful. Everything about her was light and graceful from her soft curling hair to her small, delicately shaped hands. She was a very pretty, gentle girl, and her father's eyes lighted up when he saw her.

Betsy looked around uneasily when she saw the three of them in the familiar grouping.

"Where's Frances?" she asked.

"Shh, don't bother her," her mother said.

"I did already," Betsy said sadly. "This morning I was taking my dress out of the closet, and I just tried to move her white blouse out of the way, and I'm afraid it caught on the hook in my dress, and some of the lace got torn."

"Don't tell her," Mrs. Green said. "Give it to me. I'll fix it."

"She saw it, Mama. She said I did it on purpose but, Mama, I didn't. I really didn't mean to tear it."

"Shh, she's coming."

The conspirators fell apart, and when Frances entered the kitchen, her mother was filling a large platter with latkes, Betsy was setting the table, her father was drinking a glass of water over by the sink and Marv was out of the room, and on his way up the stairs to his bedroom.

It was a tiny room, only a few feet longer and wider than his bed. The door was closed as it always was. Before entering, Marv moved a sliding panel above the handle. He put his hand through, reached around and disconnected the switch that activated the burglar alarm. Once inside, he made sure to step over the blue border on the linoleum rug on his floor. Artfully painted blue, there stretched across the border a rope, which when stepped upon, released a piece of an old volley ball net suspended from the ceiling. Marv was not completely satisfied with this as a trap since the volley ball net would not really immobilize an intruder but just temporarily startle him. Besides his mother kept complaining about it. She never seemed to remember—about stepping over the rope.

There were other things hanging from the ceiling as well as the net. Since the room was so small, Marv had rigged up an arrangement of baskets and buckets to hold books, stationery, tools and assorted unfinished projects. The basket holding the projects had been lowered and was swaying slightly, emptied and without ballast. It reminded Marv that he had removed from it, earlier that day, the clock which he had been disemboweling in the kitchen when Frances arrived. It was still in the bag of oranges in the refrigerator. He ought to go and get it now before his mother, or worse yet, Frances, discovered it. He never should have taken the clock apart in the kitchen in the first place. But he had wanted to compare the placement of its alarm to the one in the kitchen clock, and had grown so interested once he had done so that he just couldn't wait to go back to his own room.

Not that there was any reason why he should not be taking this particular clock apart. He had found it on top of a garbage can on Hoe Avenue earlier that week, and was anxious to have a look at the ratchet movement. There was something about that ratchet movement that kept bobbing up in his mind, some importance that he hadn't as yet penetrated.

He ought to go and retrieve the clock from the refrigerator, and yet . . . he looked hungrily around the room—at all his projects in progress—the crystal radio; the marble pinball machine; the combination sandwich, milk and comic book holder; and his turn-table fly trap. He'd been busy all day without a chance to even get out to the garden. The clock could wait.

He sat down on his bed and thought about what first. It was still light outside, and the bulky upside down bleach bottle caught his eye. After two days of rain, he could see the bottle held a considerable amount of water. He hurried to the window and checked. Sure enough, it was nearly a quarter full. The bottom of the bottle had been cut off to allow the rain to fall inside. A long piece of rubber tubing from an old enema bag, with its stop clip, was attached over the neck of the bottle. Marv brought the hose into the room and held it over a droopy plant of uncertain genus. He released the clip, and a refreshing gush of pure rain water flooded the plant. Marv pressed the clip again, and pushed it outside.

From the window, he had a fine view of the garden. Since no flowers grew, garden was not exactly the most descriptive word for what was happening down there. But Frances insisted on calling it a garden. Theoretically the garden belonged to everybody in the Green family but in reality there was only one gardener, and he stood, looking down at it now contentedly. The garden was where Marv spent most of his time—at least a couple of hours every day, weather permitting. The garden was where his dreams and doodles took shape. It had been his for as long as he could remember, and there were few spots in it that were bare of something built or something building.

A pair of doors lay on one side of the garden, waiting for him. He had hoped to get started on them today, but between the clock and Frances, he had been sidetracked. Now it was too late. His mother would be calling him down to supper in a few minutes.

He sat down at his combination desk, work table and put on the earphones attached to his crystal radio. He moved the wire across the face of the galena crystal, until faintly he could hear, all together, a number of stations—music from WNYC, the cheerful voice of Uncle Don on WOR, and a news program on WJZ. He needed a selector coil, and then perhaps the stations would come in separately. Tomorrow he'd better go to the radio store and see if Mr. Collins would give him an old one in exchange for running errands. He picked up his fountain pen, which was really two fountain pens, facing in opposite directions and held together by the thumb off an old rubber glove. When one pen ran out of ink, you simply turned it upside down, and used the other pen. When that ran out of ink, you filled both pens at the same time, and had, of course, twice as long a span to write.

He wrote *get a sellector coil tomorrow at r. store.*

"Ha, ha, ha," laughed Uncle Don. "It's Mary Jean Peterson's birthday. She's five years old, and Mary Jean, if you look under the couch, you'll find . . ."

". . . out on strike. John L. Lewis of the United Mineworkers says . . ."

"Yessir that's my baby . . ."

"Dum, dum, dee, da, dee, da," hummed Marv, safe at last.

4

"We hold these truths to be self-evident that all men are created equal," read Mr. Henderson, Marv's teacher in 8A^2. His nose twitched like a rabbit's sensing trouble, and he looked up from his book in time to see Frank Scacalossi duck under his desk as a cardboard bullet whizzed over his head.

"Who did that?" Mr. Henderson shrilled.

Silence.

"Who did that?" repeated Mr. Henderson, looking straight at Harriet Kahn. Harriet Kahn rose, tossed her long curls until they rippled down her back, and began wriggling cooperatively. Harriet had been wriggling and tattletaling since kindergarten, and a soft moan could be heard from the left hand back corner of the room.

"It was Ralph Crespi, Mr. Henderson. He has one of those wooden guns the boys make out of orange crates. My mother says you can take somebody's eye out with one of them."

"Ralph!"

A slim boy with innocent blue eyes rose from the last seat in the fifth row.

"Yes, Mr. Henderson?"

"Give it to me."

"Give what to you, Mr. Henderson?"

"Ralph," said Mr. Henderson, "unless you give me that gun this minute, I will send another note home to your mother, and I think I know what she plans on doing if she receives one more note from me."

Ralph reached into the interior of his desk, and extracted the article in question. "It's not mine," he said earnestly. "It was just laying here on my desk, and . . ."

"Lying on my desk," Mr. Henderson corrected. "Bring it up here!"

The gun changed hands. "It's not mine," Ralph repeated.

Mr. Henderson held the weapon in his hand, and examined it in surprise. He was used to appropriating wooden guns, made by the boys in his class, particularly in the spring. The guns had a rubber band stretched across the top, and attached to an exposed cutaway tongue in groove joint at the back. When the rubber band was released, it sent a cardboard projectile whizzing off. But this gun was far more effective than the average. It had three tops attached to one handle, and was thus capable of firing three cardboard pellets at one time.

"Now who ever thought up something like this?" mused Mr. Henderson.

Harriet Kahn was on her feet again, curls rippling, body wriggling. "It was Marv Green, Mr. Henderson."

Even though Marv tried to explain that he hadn't planned on using it against human targets, and had constructed it merely to see if it was possible to shoot off three bullets simultaneously by means of a trigger arrangement that tripped all three rubber bands at the same time, Mr. Henderson remained inflexible.

"You boys are becoming an absolute menace. A thing like this can hurt somebody very badly. I'm going to send notes home to both your parents."

"But you said," cried Ralph Crespi, "that you wouldn't send it if I gave you the gun."

"Did I?" said Mr. Henderson. "Well then, I won't if I can get a promise from you that you will never shoot one of these things off in school again."

Ralph promised.

"And I'd like it in writing please. One hundred times by tomorrow. But I am going to send a note home with Marvin because he was really responsible for making the gun, and bringing it in to school. Now I don't want to hear another word on the subject. We're supposed to be talking about the Declaration of Independence this morning, and not wasting time on garbage."

True to his word, Mr. Henderson threw the gun into the trash can where at least fifteen sets of male eyes noted it, and planned accordingly.

Marv could have explained to Mr. Henderson that Ralph had actually commissioned the making of the gun. It had been delivered that morning, and payment received in the form of four stove bolts and two water valves from Ralph's father's hardware store. But there was a special look of pleading in Ralph's eyes which Marv understood and acknowledged by remaining silent. Ralph's mother had said that if she received one more note home from school, she would not allow Ralph to deliver the *Daily News* any more. Even though Marv's mother received a goodly number of notes herself she never threatened any action. It was only when Frances saw them that the situation grew unpleasant.

So he nodded reassuringly at Ralph, put his history book on his desk, and tried to concentrate deeply on what his teacher was saying.

There was a picture in the book which showed a group of men in wigs and short pants standing around a table. Behind them sat a whole bunch of other men with wigs and short pants who were watching them attentively. The description under the illustration read: *This painting of the signing of the Declaration of Independence was made by the American artist, John Trumbull, 1756–1843.*

". . . Independence Hall in Philadelphia on July 4, 1776, Congress approved the Declaration of Independence," Mr. Henderson was saying, his voice mellow, "and the great experiment in democracy began. Our Declaration of Independence was a source of inspiration to other countries yearning for freedom."

Marv dipped his pen into the inkwell on his desk, and wrote in his notebook, *Decklaration of I.—sauce of inspira—*There was not enough ink on the pen to finish the word. He looked into the inkwell, and found it nearly empty. There was possibly enough ink though for him to finish his word.

—tion, he wrote.

Maybe during recess, he could ask Mr. Henderson to let him fill his inkwell, and perhaps Mr. Henderson would let him fill the other inkwells too. Marv found it an extremely satisfying job, carrying the bottle with its deep blue contents from desk to desk, and holding the spout over each of the thirsty glass inkwells.

"If these men, who knew they faced imprisonment and even death on the charge of treason had not had the courage to sign the Declaration of Independence, our country might still be part of England today."

Courage, thought Marv, and ink.

He studied the picture in the text book. There was a quill pen resting in an inkwell, but the picture did not show clearly how much ink there was in the inkwell.

Marv looked at all the people gathered around the table—maybe there were ten on all sides. He studied the number of men seated who would shortly be on their feet, also prepared to sign—maybe another forty or fifty. He felt a chill run down his spine. Suppose there had not been enough ink in the inkwell. Suppose it had been dry like his own.

Mr. Henderson was smiling. "The first was John Hancock, president of the Continental Congress." The teacher chuckled. "He is supposed to have said that he would sign his name so large that King George wouldn't need his spectacles to see it."

A replica of the Declaration of Independence was shown on the page next to the illustration. Look at the size of John Hancock's signature! Look at all those extra twists and twirls! Marv began to feel panicky. Why, it would take every bit of ink in his inkwell, and maybe more just to supply John Hancock alone, with enough to sign his name.

He felt a mounting irritation with John Hancock. Studying the other signatures on the Declaration showed him that there were some, like Elbridge Gerry and John Morton, not to mention several others whose names he couldn't make out, who had a little more concern for the ink consumption than John Hancock.

48

It seemed to Marv that John Hancock might have been a great patriot, and a brave fighter for freedom and all that, but he certainly didn't understand that this country wouldn't be here today if everybody had the same wasteful attitude toward ink that he did.

Wasn't there that poem they had been studying this term about how a whole war was lost just because of one horseshoe nail that didn't fit right? The horse couldn't run, the rider couldn't deliver his message, the general didn't know where the battle was supposed to be—it was a mess. Same thing though with the ink. If they had run out of ink, and if there had been no ink anywhere else in the building, and if they had to send out for some, and if the British soldiers had seen them, and grown suspicious, they might have arrested all of them. The war would never have been fought. This would still be a colony of England, and he, Marv, had no intention of letting that happen.

He squinted at the inkwell in the picture, but it was impossible to see just how much ink there was in that inkwell. All right, then, figure the worst. Figure that there was only enough for John Hancock to sign his name. Then what?

Perhaps some brave person, not an important delegate, but someone who was willing to run the risk of danger might volunteer to go out and find some ink.

A shadowy, muffled figure crept by a British soldier, dozing over his rifle. It was night. The muffled figure had something bulky concealed under his cloak. Silently he passed through the shadows and into a house with curtains drawn. Inside, there was a group of men with wigs and short pants, gathered around a table. Behind them sat a whole bunch of other men with wigs and short pants who were watching them attentively. Into their midst strode the muffled figure. He threw off his cloak. It was Marv, in a wig and short pants, holding a bottle of ink with a spout, just like the one they used in school.

Ridiculous! His face grew warm. How could he be so silly! He dismissed the apparition from the painting, and concentrated on the inkwell. How could it be kept full of ink? How?

His face wrinkled painfully over the painting. The inkwell rested on a table covered by a tablecloth. You couldn't see what was under the table. It was possible to conceal a large bottle of ink, and perhaps to have rubber tubing, not unlike his mechanism for watering his plant, attached from the bottle of ink up to the inkwell.

Yes, but it was one thing to get fluid to flow down. How did you get it to flow up? Marv pressed his lips together, and sank his head in his hands. How could you get the ink to flow up from the bottle to the inkwell? Up. That was the key word. But what was the problem? Why did he always make things harder than they really were. If you want something to flow up, you attach a pump. Nothing complicated about that.

Now then, that problem was solved. Or was it? What was to prevent the bottle of ink under the table from running out of ink? Marv hit his head. Shortsighted as usual. No, he needed a greater source of supply. How about in the cellar of Independence Hall? How about a vat of ink, like one of those huge wine barrels? That could hold enough ink to last for a couple of years. Sure, you could even rig it up so that when the ink dropped below a certain level, a spring loaded pendulum could begin banging against a couple of pails. You would still have enough ink left for a few days when that happened, so that even if all the signers of the Declaration of Independence heard the banging, they still wouldn't have to worry about going out to find some ink.

Marv leaned his cheek on his hand, and thought with satisfaction how nothing in this world is impossible if you put your mind to it.

Of course, with the vat in the basement of Independence Hall, you could have pipes running into every room in the building. Pipes could connect with every inkwell in the place. No inkwell in Independence Hall need ever run dry again. Marv licked his lips. But wait! Pipes? Were there any pipes in 1776? Maybe not, but there are today. All over the country, important papers have to be signed. John Hancock wasn't the only one who needed ink. How about President Roosevelt? Didn't he need ink? And Governor Lehman? And Mayor La Guardia?

All over the country, people had electricity, didn't they? They had water pumped in and out of their houses. How about ink? Wouldn't people always need ink? Didn't his own father need ink? What would the Bakers Union, Local 27 do if his father didn't have enough ink to write his reports? Nobody should ever be without ink. Every city should have a central supply with pipes that connected to every house. The ink could flow forever, and this country would be safe.

But where was everybody going? Why was everybody getting up? He wasn't finished. He hadn't worked out ink meters for each house. Why was everybody in such a hurry?

"Marvin," said Mr. Henderson, "didn't you even hear the three o'clock bell?"

Marv shook his head, trying to shake himself back into P.S. 63 at three o'clock on a Friday afternoon, April 30, 1940.

"Marvin," said Mr. Henderson, writing something at his desk, "will you please take this home, and ask your mother to sign it. I want you to bring it back on Monday." He put the note in an envelope, sealed it, and held it out to Marv.

"When I think," he said as Marv took the note, "that you are Frances Green's brother, I am struck with amazement."

"I know," Marv said. "She's not happy about it either."

"I will admit," Mr. Henderson continued, "that I

have seldom had a student like Frances. Any teacher would glory in a student like Frances. But take Betsy now—not as good a student as Frances, certainly, but willing and cooperative. The important thing, Marvin, is she tried. Anybody can try." He put his arm on Marv's shoulder. "A person doesn't have to be brilliant like Frances to try."

Marv knew Mr. Henderson was being patient and kind. He nodded and smiled to show Mr. Henderson he appreciated his interest.

Mr. Henderson said, "You have to try, Marvin, try to keep your mind on your work. Every time I look at you, you're doodling or daydreaming. Today, for instance, what were you thinking about? Aren't you at all interested in your country's history? Don't you take any pride at all in the courage of those patriots? What was so important that you had to think about it instead of the Declaration of Independence?"

Mr. Henderson's rimless glasses with eyes behind them were very close to Marv's face. What was he going to say to Mr. Henderson? "I was thinking about ink, Mr. Henderson?"

"Nothing," Marv said finally.

"That's what I thought," said the teacher. "That's all you ever seem to think about. Nothing."

5

At about 6:15 A.M., Saturday morning, Marv was standing thoughtfully in the center of the garden. A sparrow in the ailanthus tree at the back was singing with all its heart, a little, bewildered tulip was poking its head up from the ground not a foot away from where he stood, and pink and orange clouds still frosted the early morning sky. Marv was unaware of any of these distractions.

All his thoughts were directed at an object in front of him—a pair of revolving doors made out of four halves of two old doors. Revolving doors should revolve easily, not groan and hardly budge when you pushed them. Marv leaned with all his might on the door on his left. He felt a slight movement, and prodded the door with his elbow. It moved, very slowly, with a rasping screech of protest. No, no, he had better take the doors down, and plane the bottoms, because they were still scraping along the ground.

While he was involved in taking them down, he became aware of the tulip. It was after he had stepped on it while pulling the doors along the ground to the steps. The little mashed bud was not a pleasing sight, and there was something about it which stirred a forgotten memory. At the moment, however, with the heavy doors to handle, he could not take the time to remember.

A few hours later, his memory was refreshed. Frances came through the basement, carrying a canvas folding chair, and a book. She was smiling agreeably, and Marv knew it was going to be one of those days. Of course, Frances had as much right to the garden as he had, and on days like this, why shouldn't she come out and read? He looked up hopefully, but there was not one single, little cloud in the clear blue sky.

"Good morning, Marv," Frances said cheerfully.

"Good morning, Frances." It was probably going to be even worse than he had thought.

"Where are you working? I don't want to disturb you. Just go right ahead, and don't even notice me."

Frances stepped over the mound on the right, which contained some of the most ancient relics the garden offered. As a matter of fact, the layer at the very bottom of the mound could be dated somewhere back to 1930, when a four-year-old Marv pushed a nail through the bottom of an empty Dixie cup, and made an upside down umbrella. Above that specimen, came a later but still ancient artifact from Marv's fifth year, when paper gave way to wood, and a little bed for a headless toy rabbit had been constructed out of a cheese box and four nails. The top layers, which seemed to the untrained eye a pile of junk, contained rich deposits of past projects. Similar mounds lay in other parts of the garden, and Frances moved warily among them.

Between the mound containing the remains of a bicycle built for three cats, and the large, large mound containing an attempt at a domed kiosk, Frances found a level spot. She opened her chair, sat down in it, sniffed the warm, spring air, smiled kindly at Marv, opened her book, and began to read.

It would not last, Marv knew, but with whatever time was left to him, he turned his attention once more to the doors. The problem right now was that they spun so fast, you had to run very hard not to get whacked. They needed to be slowed down, but how? It was just as he began thinking about that ratchet movement inside the clock, and its possible relevance here when Frances spoke.

"What are you making?" She was looking at him from over her book, and her voice was sweet.

"Revolving doors," he said carefully.

"My," she said, "isn't that an unusual idea." She resumed reading, and Marv watched and waited. She turned a page, so he turned his attention back to the relevance of the ratchet movement.

What was its function inside the clock? Think, you dope, think. Its function was to regulate the movement of the hands. Marv began to grow excited.

"But why revolving doors?"

"What?"

"Why revolving doors?" Frances put down her book, "I mean, people put revolving doors in a building. They have a function in a building. They let people in, and they let them out—but if—you're already out, and not going to be going in, I mean, Marv, why revolving doors?" Frances' smile was still kind, but there was a familiar look around the eyes.

"I dunno," said Marv.

"I see." Frances nodded encouragingly at him, picked up her book again, and read. This time he waited until she turned two pages before returning to the question of that ratchet movement. Now then. He agreed it regulated the movement of the hands from going too fast or too slow. Yes, of course, wher-

ever you wanted to regulate movement, a ratchet arrangement could . . ."

"It's like putting in a window, but leaving off the
house, or putting in a faucet without a pipe. Don't
you see, Marv, it doesn't do anything."

"Huh?"

"Listen, will you, and try not to look so—well, never
mind." Frances took a deep breath, and fanned the
smile a little until it jelled once more—a little shaky on
the ends perhaps, but holding in the middle.

"Come here, Marv, I want to talk to you."

Marv thought, I could tell her not right now. I'm
busy now. Maybe later. I could say I'm right in the
middle of something, and come back later. I don't have
to if I don't want to. I can say no.

He walked over to Frances. She patted the long part
of her chair, and Marv sat down on it.

"Look around this garden, Marv. What do you see?"

Marv looked. "I dunno," he said.

"Shall I tell you what I see?"

"Uh, Frances, maybe a little later you could . . ."

"I see," said Frances sweetly, "a mess. I see a whole
bunch of unfinished, useless, hideous, screwball projects."

". . . maybe later . . ."

"For years now you've been dragging all kinds of
garbage into this garden, and banging and building,
and what have you made?" Her hand moved in a
complete circle. "A mess. Nothing else."

As Frances went on talking, Marv became absorbed in watching her teeth. How fast they were moving. A ratchet now . . . on Frances' mouth . . .

"Well—have you?"

"What?"

"I asked," said Frances' teeth, moving very fast, "if you ever, in your whole life, finished one thing?"

"I finished lots of things," Marv protested.

"Like what?"

"Well—I made that dog house for Queenie."

"But you never put a roof on it. And besides, you know she sleeps under the stove. Why should you make a house for her in the first place? That's just typical of the way your mind works." She put a hand on his arm, and said earnestly, "You know something, Marv, I don't really think you're stupid."

This was the first nice thing she had ever really said to him. His mouth fell open even wider than it already was. She looked at it in distaste, and then said quickly, "Shut your mouth, will you. And how come you never comb your hair, and just look at your neck."

This was more like it, and he felt a little more comfortable. But Frances stopped suddenly, swallowed hard, and continued in that strained, sweet voice.

"No, if I thought you were completely stupid, I wouldn't even bother talking to you. You notice, I never bother with Betsy."

Marv considered this statement, which did not seem to him completely accurate.

"I think there's more to you than perhaps I've given you credit for. You are handy, I must say, even if you never seem to use it for anything useful. Only to make trouble, and now—to hurt people."

So she knew. Marv watched her pull out the note from her book, and read it to herself. "Guns," she said, "my brother making guns."

"Listen, Frances, I can explain about that," Marv cried, "I wasn't making that gun to use on anybody. I just wanted to see if I could develop a more effective trigger mechanism. It just happened that Ralph heard me talking about it, and asked me to make one for him. But I never was planning to use it on anybody."

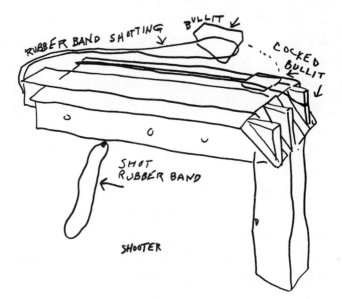

"Was he?"

"Who?"

"Ralph."

"I guess so, but I had nothing to do with him."

"No, you just masterminded the whole thing, designed a much more effective weapon, put it into the hands of someone who might never have used one, and you're trying to tell me that your responsibility ended after you made the gun. If it was used to hurt someone, nobody could blame you. Is that what you're saying?"

"But, Frances, it was only one of those wooden guns that shoots cardboard pieces. It couldn't really hurt anybody."

"You know who you remind me of," said Frances, really hot now, and not waiting for him to answer. "You remind me of those Nazi scientists in Germany, working for Hitler. They're supposed to be working on pure science, but somehow out of their research, the most deadly weapons come to kill and cripple and destroy. I'm sure they don't think they're responsible either."

She read the note again, and shook her head. "Guns and daydreams," she said. "They just don't go together. Out of daydreams should come poetry and music and beautiful, beautiful things. Great scientific truths and discoveries that will help people, not hurt them." Frances' voice was shaking. "You may not know this, Marv, but I daydream too, and I'll tell you what

I daydream about. One day I'll be finished with school, and I daydream about when that day comes, and I'm a doctor, I'll go to China where the people are dying from war and disease and famine. Even if there still is a war on, I'm going to China, and I'm going to help those people, and I don't care what happens to me. I'm going to help."

For a moment, while she sat there, her face tight and her fist clenched, Marv looked at her with admiration. She was splendid, magnificent, this supersister of his, this brilliant Frances who would be the doctor every Jewish family was supposed to want their boy to be, and his family knew their boy could never manage to be. But their daughter would. This admirable, noble, genius sister of his, and he felt so sorry for her suddenly, he patted her arm without thinking, and murmured, "That's all right, Frances. It's going to be all right."

Did she turn on him then!

"And who do you think about helping, you fascist you? Guns! You make guns! Do you ever think about making anything useful? Monster! Can you make anything besides guns?" She put her face up close to his, and cried, "Do you ever read the paper? Do you know what's happening in Europe? Do you know about Hitler? That's what he daydreams about—guns. Just like you. Is that what you're going to be like when you grow up?"

Bong, bong, bong, bong.

"No, no," Marv cried in horror. "I won't make any more guns. You're right, Frances. I'll never make another one."

"It's not enough," Frances said relentlessly, "not to do something wrong. How about doing something right."

"What do you want me to do, Frances? I'll do anything you want me to do."

"Stop ruining my flowers," she cried. "Didn't I plant tulip bulbs last fall? Didn't I tell you that I was planting them? Didn't I ask you to be careful of them?" She looked around the garden furiously. "I don't even know where I planted them now. You've thrown so much junk around, it's impossible to have any kind of bearings."

Very casually, Marv stood up, slowly ambled over to where the mashed tulip bud lay, and put his foot over it.

"Why don't you do something with whatever abilities you've got. You're always starting a million things and never finishing anything. Finish something for a change. Make something that will benefit somebody."

"I made that mudguard in front of the door," Marv said humbly. It may not have been much, but it was something he had done to benefit somebody.

"Yes," replied Frances, "and if you're really going to do something useful, you can start by taking it away. I fell over it the other day when I was carrying a load of books, and did you see that bruise on Mama's knee? All right, all right, you don't have to look as if you haven't got a friend in the world."

She stood up, walked over to him, and shook his shoulder. Her face was friendly. He was only afraid he would lose his balance, and she would see the dead tulip.

"What do you want me to do after I take away the mudguard?"

"Marv," Frances said, "where do you generally get your ideas from?"

"Huh?"

"What makes you decide to make revolving doors, or a roofless dog house?"

Marv looked down at his foot. A bit of green showed left of his instep. He moved it slightly, and said, "I guess it's when I find something—like I found both of those doors when they took down the market on Jennings Street. And I made the dog house because Sam Fink's father makes chairs, and he threw out those spiral spokes, and . . ."

"How about starting the other way? Start with the thing itself. Decide to make something that somebody needs, and then get the materials."

"What do you need, Frances? I'll make you something you need."

Frances was smiling. She was pretty when she smiled.

"No, this is going to be up to you. I'm not going to tell you. You'll have to figure it out for yourself. You think of something somebody needs. It doesn't have to be me. How about Mama? Why don't you make something for Mama?"

"I will. But what?"

"Marv, you have a brain. Everybody has a brain, so use it."

Two compliments in one day from Frances. Marv squirmed in embarrassment.

"Why don't you go to the library? That's a good place to develop ideas. Look in some of the mechanical books or the craft books. A boy like you should learn to use the library."

Bong, bong, bong, bong.

"I'll go right now, Frances. I'm on my way. You're right, Frances. It'll be different from now on. I'll see you later. You won't be disappointed, Frances."

It was such a sweet smile, almost like his mother's when he ate a lot of food. He looked over his shoulder just as he was going through the basement door to wave at her—his brilliant, *smiling* sister.

But her eyes were focusing on a broken bit of green on the ground. The smile had vanished, and he did not stay to inquire where it had gone.

6

A cardboard bullet whizzed past his left ear, and came to land on a stack of *Daily News* on the ground in front of Drexler's Candy Store. The cardboard dropped just above a picture of Norwegian soldiers waving from the window of a train. The headline said NORWAY FIGHTS BACK.

He heard snickering, and turned to see Ralph Crespi and Frank Scacalossi sitting on the stoop of Ralph's house. Frank was waving the three-powered wooden gun Marv had last seen in Mr. Henderson's wastebasket.

"Over here, Marv!"

"I can't. I'm going somewhere."

"Come *on!*"

For a minute then. He walked over to them. He could hear Ralph talking angrily to Frank as he approached. "Go ahead, ask him and see if he thinks it's fair."

"I don't have to ask him," Frank said cheerfully. "Finders keepers, losers weepers. I got there first during the lunch hour, and I fished it out so now it's mine."

"That's not fair," Ralph cried. "I paid him for it, and it's mine. You know it's mine. If you want one, ask him to make one for you."

"OK, OK." Frank tossed the gun to Ralph. "Make me one, Marv. What do you want for it?"

"I can't." Marv sat down on the steps.

"I'll give you a dime."

"I can't."

"All right—fifteen cents, but that's all."

"Look—I mean it. I can't."

Silence.

"How come," Frank finally said, "you can make him one, and not me? I even let you copy off me on the history test Thursday."

"I promised Frances."

"I won't tell."

"No. She's right." Marv stood up. "I'm not going to make any more guns. From now on, I'm only going to make things to help people, not to hurt them. Good-bye!"

Ralph made a choking sound in his throat, but Frank said quickly, "OK, OK, but let's talk it over. Sit down. Where are you going in such a hurry? I never see you any more. You're always busy."

"I'm going to the library."

"What for?"

"I promised Frances I'd look up something useful to make from one of the books."

Frank whistled, and Ralph again made the choking noise, but this time, combined with another noise that sounded like vomiting. Put like that his intentions did sound nutty. He hesitated, and Frank said gently, "You poor creep. Why don't you get her married?"

"Who to?"

Frank thought hard. "You're right. Who'd marry her?"

Faint stirrings of family honor. A boy should defend his sister's good name. "Hey, cut it out, Frank. She's not so bad." Marv sat down again. His friends' sympathetic faces were unsettling.

"She's right though." Marv tried again. "She says all this killing has to stop. People should be building beautiful things to help one another, not . . ." He looked gloomily at the gun, his creation, lying in Ralph's lap.

"It's that crazy Hitler," said Frank. "He started the

whole war—first he invaded Austria, then Czechoslovakia, Poland, and now Denmark."

"But they'll beat him in Norway," Ralph said confidently. "My father said the German Navy is no match for England's."

Frank shook his head. "My father said he'll take Norway, and that he won't be satisfied until he has all of Europe."

"Say," Ralph said, "did you see the paper this morning?"

Marv stood up. "I'm going."

"No, wait. Did you see how some guy offered a million dollars to anybody who captures Hitler?"

Marv began walking off. "I'll see you later."

"Listen, dope, listen! You want to do something good, how about capturing Hitler? Come on, let's go over to Drexler's. I'll show you it in the paper."

The three of them crossed the street, and hovered over the newspapers on the stand outside the candy store. Ralph picked up a copy of the *Times,* and pointed to the headline right in the middle of page one.

$1,000,000 OFFERED FOR CAPTURE OF HITLER ALIVE

The offer had been made by the president of the Carnegie Institute, who issued the following statement:

"In order to prevent further bloodshed and outrage in this war of the German aggression, I am authorized by competent Americans to offer a reward of $1,000-

ooo to be paid in cash to the person or persons who will deliver Adolf Hitler, alive, unwounded, and unhurt into the custody of the League of Nations for trail before a high court of justice for his crimes against the peace and dignity of the world. This proposal will stand good through the month of May 1940."

"Persons." Frank pointed to the word. "It doesn't have to be one person."

"The month of May. That's not much time." Ralph leaned against the stand, and looked at Marv. "Do you think we could?"

"Are you boys buying a newspaper?" asked Mr. Drexler, all 218 pounds of him emerging from the candy store. "Or are you making me come out for nothing?"

"Should I buy a newspaper?" asked Frank. "I've got three cents."

"What for?" said Ralph. "We read it already. Why don't you go and buy something we can eat."

A few minutes later, the three boys, chewing on caramels, were walking thoughtfully down Franklin Avenue.

"First you've got to get over there," Frank pointed out to Ralph.

"No problem. You stow away."

"OK, then once you're there, you've got to get by his guards."

"Couldn't we say we want to see him? Wouldn't

they let three kids get in? Nobody would suspect three kids, would they?"

"Ralph, how can you be so dumb?" said Frank. "Who's going to say we want to see him? Who can talk German?"

"Marv can."

"No, I can't."

"I always hear your parents talking German. Sometimes you talk to them in German."

"That's Yiddish, not German."

"It sounds the same. Couldn't you get away with it if you talked real low, and maybe stuttered? German kids stutter too. They'd think you had a speech problem."

"Well, maybe. But even if we did get in to see him. Then what? What do we tell him? And how do we get him out?"

Nobody said anything for a while. Then Marv began fidgeting. The two boys looked at him, and waited. The fidgeting increased.

"Marv?" Frank questioned softly.

"I think . . . I know how."

Three German boys, three boys anyway who looked German—blond hair (bleached), blue eyes (two had blue eyes. The one who spoke German wore sunglasses.)—clicked their heels smartly before the guard, and made the familiar raised arm salute.

"Heil Hitler," said the one who wore glasses.

"Heil Hitler," snapped the guard. "What do you want?" (He spoke in German, naturally.)

"We w-w-want to see the Fuehrer."

"What was that, boy? Can't you speak properly?"

"We want to see the Fuehrer."

"Do you have an appointment?"

"No, but we have a secret weapon."

"What did you say? A secret weapon? I can't understand you. One of you other boys better speak."

But the other two boys, pointing to the mufflers around their necks, and emitting hoarse noises from their mouths, made it plain that for some reason, they were unable to speak.

"Very strange," said the guard suspiciously, his hand moving toward the gun at his belt.

The one with glasses—it was Marv—quickly unwrapped a model, and showed it to the guard.

"Gott in Himmel!" cried the guard, staggering back. "Wait here."

In a few minutes, an escort of ten huge, blond storm troopers escorted the three boys through room after room, containing monocled German officers who clicked their heels, and shouted "Heil Hitler" at the marchers.

Finally, they reached a door, black and ugly, with one ornament, an evil-looking, blood red swastika right in the center. One of the officers tapped on the door, and a high-pitched voice shouted, "Come!"

The door opened, and the three boys were escorted

inside. Hitler, surrounded by two generals, sat at a huge desk. He was even uglier than his pictures, and his uniform was too big for him. His boots had high heels, to make him look taller.

Everybody shouted "Heil Hitler," and there was a loud heel-clicking sound.

"Come here," he ordered the boys. He waved his hand in dismissal, and the soldiers all left. The boys were alone with Hitler and his two generals.

"What is this about a secret weapon? Let me see."

Marv placed the model on the desk, and unwrapped it.

"Gott in Himmel!" said Hitler. "My own scientists have not been able to develop a rocket, and you, a mere boy . . ." His eyes narrowed. "How do we know it works?" He looked at the tallest, blue-eyed, blond boy—Frank Scacalossi, alias Franz Schumannkraut—who coughed helplessly, and tugged at his muffler.

"I must answer for my comrades," Marv stuttered, "who are unable to speak after being tortured by our country's enemies, and screaming for hours that they would not divulge any secrets. They did not scream out of pain, but out of defiance. So now, they have temporarily lost their voices."

"And you?" questioned the Fuehrer, his eyes like evil slits of yellow light. "You speak very strangely, but why is it that your voice is not gone?"

Marv clicked his heels together. "I endured the torture without crying defiance because I knew we would escape, and that my voice would be needed to explain to our Fuehrer how the rocket works."

"Brave German boys," said the Fuehrer. "And how does it work?"

"I will need a metal table to demonstrate it properly."

"Go!" commanded Hitler. One of the generals left the room.

"And one pail of hot water . . . and one pail of cold."

"Go!"

The second general left the room. Marv approached the Fuehrer, and began explaining the principles of rocketry to him. Hitler was so absorbed in listening, and looking at the model that he did not notice at first what the other two boys were doing. The taller one began moving carefully behind him, while the other boy backed up to the door, and locked it.

A sudden movement behind him, and Hitler cried, "What are you doing?" But it was too late. A veil of chloroform was clamped over his face, and Marv hurried to help Frank hold the thrashing arms and kicking feet. Ralph paid no attention to the struggling group, but systematically began prodding the molding on one wall.

A few muffled moans, one or two more feeble movements, and the chloroform did its work. Adolf Hitler, would-be-conqueror-of-the-world, collapsed and lay sprawling at their feet.

"Here it is," said Ralph, whose practiced fingers had found the button that opened the bookcase, and led into the secret tunnel.

A tap on the door, and Marv shouted in a perfect imitation of the Fuehrer, "Go away! I want to be alone."

They dragged the unconscious figure into the tunnel to the car which they knew would be waiting there. They opened the trunk of the car, deposited Hitler inside, locked it securely, jumped into the front, and sped off through the tunnel, out into the bright sunlight where two guards fired guns after them, raced madly through the countryside with hundreds of cars after them, and made it over the French border just as their car ran out of gasoline.

"No good," Marv said.

"Why not?" Ralph's voice was still hoarse, his eyes blinking, his fists clenched.

Frank's eyes were glazed from listening. "Why not?" he said dreamily. "We made it over the border. Nothing can stop us now."

"But nobody drives," Marv said.

"Couldn't you learn?"

"With only a month? I've got to make the model of the rocket, and brush up on my German. Then we've got to get over there and back."

"Maybe I could learn," said Ralph.

"Maybe."

They walked on up 168th Street, silently considering the one straw, the one fly, the one unsolvable problem that lay between them and the capture of Adolf Hitler.

"Maybe I *could* learn," Ralph insisted.

But they all knew he could not.

"I guess I'll go on to the library," said Marv. "See you guys later."

He walked off by himself, and after a second or two, he heard Frank call, "Marv!"

"What?" He looked back over his shoulder. Frank was holding up the gun. "Will you do it for twenty cents?"

"No." He began walking again.

"Marv."

"What?"

"For twenty-five?"

He took a deep breath, and ran as fast as he could to the library.

7

The Boys Book of Manual Arts and *The Boy Craftsman* contained a great number of projects a boy like himself could easily build. Both books had explicit instructions and no end of drawings, diagrams, photographs and shopping lists of precisely what was needed, and where a boy should go to obtain the familiar, inexpensive, easily accessible materials. He agreed wholeheartedly with the statement in *Boys Book of Manual Arts* that "One need not purchase expensive materials or rare tools to fashion articles of distinction." Neither could he find anything to disagree with in the opening sentence of *The Boy Craftsman* that "Of all the experiences in life, there is nothing that offers the growing boy more satisfaction than forging a good piece of work with his own two hands."

It was not until he was halfway through the first book that he began to feel troubled. By the time he was halfway through the second, his own limitations struck him with full force.

Here he was, looking at a wealth of beautiful, useful items to make. It was not just a matter of one or two or even twenty or thirty. He had been turning hundreds of pages in the last hour or so, and nothing happened. In the past, whenever he decided to make something he never had to sit and think do I want to make this or don't I want to make that? There would be a stirring in him, a rippling, and then there he would be, working. How come, now, after looking at all these beautiful, useful things—certainly more beautiful and useful than anything he'd ever made— he was still sitting, not working, and nothing was happening inside him?

He knew it was not the fault of the books. People who write books know what they are doing. He flipped through the pages of the second book and stopped at a photograph of a two-tiered flower stand on wheels that could be moved from one sunny window to another. A smiling matron, younger and thinner than his mother, was pictured watering a group of blooming flowers. Now here was something that any woman would probably love to have. His own mother did not have too many plants, but she watered the ones she had every day and seemed to be fond of them. There was the big snake plant in the living room, two cactus plants in the kitchen, and that sweet potato growing on top of the refrigerator. The snake plant was too big to fit on the cart, but the two cactus plants would fit. There would be lots of room left over. He supposed he could add the plant in his room, and maybe his mother would like to put the sweet potato on too, and weren't there any other plants in the house? Did his sisters have a plant in their room? He couldn't remember. Of course, none of them were blooming like the ones in the book, but he supposed there were places where you could get blooming plants. He tried to work up some enthusiasm for it, but there·was something lacking in himself, and nothing happened.

Well, how about the "Mandarin Coffee Table" on the next page? Even if his parents only drank coffee in the morning in the kitchen, his mother would probably be overjoyed at having such a handsome piece of furniture in the living room. He examined the photograph which showed a much larger room than his living room. There was even a piano in the room pictured in the book. He had to admit that their room, at home, was considerably smaller. With only their three piece set, his father's desk, the radio cabinet, and the snake plant, there wasn't too much room to move around. Between the couch and the snake plant,

there wasn't any room at all to move about. So where would the "Mandarin Coffee Table" go?

Apologetically, he flipped through more pages, considering sewing boxes, bookcases, tables for lamps and lamps for tables, knickknack shelves, bookends and candy dishes.

What *was* the matter with him? With all the beautiful, useful things he was looking at, why was it that there was not one single, solitary item he wanted to build? "Start with the thing itself," Frances had said. "Decide to make something that somebody needs, and then get the materials."

Of course, it was logical. Edison didn't wait until he found some wires and a glass bowl before he made a light bulb. Fulton didn't just happen to find an old tea kettle in the junkyard before he designed a steam engine. Why should it be that when he looked at a picture of a beautiful, useful thing, and then read over the materials to be purchased, he felt uncomfortable? Why was it that anything he ever made developed out of something he had found in a garbage can or on a construction site or on an empty lot?

Desperately, he flipped through the pages of his book once more, and found himself looking at a picture of a sewing box "Just for Mom." I'll make her that, he thought. Even though she does keep most of her stuff in the sewing machine cabinet, she'll like this. Look at the way that lady is smiling over it.

What would he need? He'd have to go to the lumberyard, and *buy* some clean white pine and small dowels to hold the spools in place. Marv swallowed. None of that was expensive. All right. What next. The box would have to be lined. The book suggested pink felt with a special red velvet cushion for pins. He would have to go to Woolworth's, and ask for pink felt and red velvet. "Miss," he'd have to say, "could I have some pink felt and a piece of red velvet. I'm making a sewing box for my mother."

Marv slammed the book closed, and quickly left the library. Frances was wasting her time on him. After this episode in the library, all her criticism of him seemed justified. Maybe he should just face up to it, and accept once and for all that he was the kind of person who was incapable of appreciating beauty, and would probably never be able to do anything useful for anybody.

On the way home, he found a whole coil of rope from a washline. It was lying there on 169th Street, right where the trolley stops. The rope was at least thirty feet long, and was hardly frayed.

His father was walking down the front steps when Marv arrived home. Today, being Saturday, Papa was off from work. He hurried up to him, but then slowed down when he saw the large bundle in his hand. Papa would be busy with union affairs today.

"Marv," his father greeted him. "I'm glad you're here. Could you do me a favor, and take these papers over to Ralph Needleman's house? He lives on Clinton Avenue. Do you remember, you took him some papers for me another time? 2076 Clinton Avenue? It's on the other side of the park. I have so much work to do today, and you'll save me a trip if you can go. Take the Prospect Avenue bus, and it won't take long."

"Sure, Papa," Marv said. "I'll just put this rope in the basement." He hurried through the cellar door, dropped the rope, and came back out.

His father was still standing on the steps. He had his head up, and was sniffing the air in deep, appreciative sniffs.

"Such a day," he said, "such a lovely day. I'm almost sorry I have to be stuck in."

"Papa," Marv coaxed, "why don't you stop for a while, and take a walk with me?"

"Walk?" said his father, startled.

"It's such a nice day," Marv said quickly. "We can walk through the park. Come on, Papa, please. Take a walk with me."

His father held out his arms helplessly, and shook his head. "I'd like to, Marvin," he said, "but I'm so busy."

"All right, Papa," Marv held out his hand, and his father handed him the parcel, and gave him a dime for carfare back and forth.

"I'd really like to go with you," said his father.

"That's all right, Papa. I'll be back soon."

He began walking away from the house, when his father called after him, "Marvin, wait!"

Marv turned. His father was coming down the steps. "I think I will take a walk with you," he laughed. "Why· not? All work and no play make Irving Green fat in the middle."

"Oh, Papa, you're not fat," Marv said admiringly to the pale, thin man who came quickly toward him.

"You know," said his father as they walked up Franklin Avenue to the park, "I haven't gone for a walk in the park for so long, I don't remember when."

He kept patting his son's shoulder, and taking deep gulps of the warm, spring air. Everything seemed to have turned green overnight. There were tight little buds on the trees, and some of the children climbing over the rocks and lawns, had shed their winter coverings.

"Papa," Marv said.

"Umm."

"Papa, if I wanted to make something for Mama, what would you think she'd like. I mean, what could she use?"

"Something for Mama?" His father looked puzzled.

The Green family did not go in for presents. On the children's birthdays, Mrs. Green usually baked a marble cake or a sponge cake. If there was enough money, there might be a useful present like a sweater or a shirt. But only for the children. The grownups did not acknowledge anniversaries or birthdays, and would have been surprised and embarrassed if anybody presented them with presents to mark a particular day.

"I just thought I'd like to make her something."

"I see. You mean, just like that?"

"Uh, huh."

"Very nice," said his father.

"So what should I make?"

"What should you make?"

"Yes, what should I make?"

His father thought for a few seconds, and said, "Make her something she needs."

"That's what I want to do, but what does she need?"

His father's face wrinkled thoughtfully, but he remained silent. After a few minutes, Marv said sadly, "I guess she really doesn't need anything, does she?"

His father smiled. "She's a lucky woman, your mother," he said. Then his face looked puzzled again. "I really haven't thought about it, and it's a good idea to think about what Mama needs for a change."

"What about a sewing box?"

"Maybe. Yes. I think that's a very good idea. Why don't you make her a sewing box?"

"But she keeps all her things in the sewing machine cabinet."

"That's right. She does."

"What do you think of a jewelry box?"

"Well, maybe so. Let me see, she has her wedding ring . . ."

"But she wears that."

"All right. She has a watch, and she usually doesn't wear that, and I think a locket, and . . . what else?"

"That pin with a lady's face on it."

"Yes, and . . . something else?"

"I don't know."

"Maybe she doesn't need a jewelry box," said his father.

"What about a cart for flowers?"

"What flowers?"

"How about a lamp?"

"For where?"

"For . . . anywhere."

"Do you think she needs a lamp? She sits in the kitchen at night. She doesn't need a lamp there."

"You see," said Marv, "it's a problem finding something she needs."

"I'm sure there's something she needs," his father said. "Let's both keep thinking about it, and we'll figure something out. But I think it was very nice that you thought up the idea to make Mama something."

They walked slowly along the path behind the playground, and sat down on a bench overlooking Indian Lake.

"Papa," Marv admitted, "it wasn't my idea to make Mama something."

"No? Who then?"

"Frances. It was her idea."

"Very thoughtful of Frances," said his father, leaning his head against the back of the bench, the better to feel the sun on his face.

"She's always thinking of other people," Marv said. "She thinks about how to help people. She doesn't just waste her time making ugly, useless things."

His father closed his eyes, and murmured, "No, she never wastes her time."

"She's going to be a doctor," Marv said, "and go to China, and help people."

"Mmm," said his father.

Marv looked at the thin, pale face turned up to the sun. "You help people," he said. "You make bread for people to eat. You work in the union to help other bakers have a better life. Lots of people," Marv said glumly, "help people, and don't just make a mess."

His father's eyelids flickered faintly. Through his partly opened lips, the breath came deeply. Marv stopped talking. He sat quietly on the bench for a few moments. It was not easy sitting quietly on a bench next to someone who was asleep. It was also embarrassing looking at someone who was asleep. After a few moments, he stood up, very carefully, and walked down to the lake. Two younger boys were holding a milk bottle under the water trying to catch fish. Marv showed them how to tie a rope around the neck of the bottle and suspend it in the water. By the time his father woke up, there were three fish swimming in the milk bottle, two fish in a Dixie cup found in a garbage can, and seven fish in a jar discovered in the same place.

By the time they arrived home, Mama and the girls were already eating, and they hurried to wash up and join them.

"Such a day!" beamed Mr. Green. "My son and I must have covered every square inch in Crotona Park today."

"It's good for you to get out," said Mrs. Green. "You even got a little color in your face."

"Mmm, Mama, this noodle kugel is delicious," said Betsy.

Frances said, "Did you see in the paper this morning, some joker offered a million dollars for the capture of Adolf Hitler, alive? He would be brought before the League of Nations on charges of crimes against humanity."

"Sounds like a good idea to me," said Mr. Green, looking down with pleasure at his plate heaped high with chicken, carrots, and kugel.

"Papa, you really surprise me," Frances said loftily. "You can't really think it would make one bit of difference whether there's a Hitler or not a Hitler."

"I'd be very glad if there was no Hitler," said Mr. Green.

"And that in a nutshell is the trouble with your generation," lectured Frances. "You believe in individuals and not movements. Don't you understand that if there was no Hitler, there'd be a million others to take his place—a million Nazis and fascists, a million would-be dictators. The whole world has to change," Frances cried passionately, "and then mankind will change. The old systems have to give way to the new. There has to be a new world with new goals, and one government, and anyone who thinks that Adolf Hitler, alone, is responsible for everything that's gone wrong with the world, is asleep."

Mr. Green silently ate his food, and Marv rejoiced inwardly that he did not know how to drive a car.

8

On Sunday mornings, Mrs. Green generally washed a "few things by hand." Heavy laundry, such as sheets, tablecloths, and towels were sent out for "wet wash." Dresses, blouses, underwear, nightgowns, pajamas, and any other article not classified as heavy was done "by hand."

The clothes were sorted into whites and coloreds. Then Mrs. Green filled up the bathtub with water and soap. She knelt beside it on a rubber mat, and began washing each article separately. The very lightest were done first, and as the colors of the clothes deepened so did the water in the bathtub. A small washboard was propped against the side of the tub, and Mrs. Green rubbed any particularly stubborn spot against its rippling front. The sound of the clothes as they were scrubbed against the washboard made a deep, rhythmic sound which the rest of the family could hear as they sat around the table eating breakfast.

"Every worker is exploited," Frances said, "but at least there's a limit to how many hours a person can legally work. Some people work forty hours, and even you, Papa, never work more than forty-eight. But Mama never stops. It's criminal."

"You're absolutely right," said her father looking up from his newspaper, and nodding in agreement. "But there's no way to stop her." He turned a page, and began reading again.

"There's no reason why a woman has to do all the housework herself," continued Frances. "This is supposed to be a democracy. We're supposed to believe that everybody is equal—women as well as men. Nobody believes any more that men are smarter than women. Nowadays a girl should be able to go to school, and grow up to be anything she wants—a doctor, a lawyer, an engineer—anything. Being a housewife is no career. It's sheer drudgery. No woman should be stuck doing housework all by herself. There's no reason why a man can't cook and clean and even change diapers. In a decent marriage, a man and woman should share the burdens equally."

"You're right," said her father.

"Well, why is it you never help Mama with the housework? I never, once in my whole life, saw you do the dishes," Frances said hotly. "Papa, you have a double standard. No matter what you say you really believe that women are inferior."

Her father put his paper down. "No, Frances," he said earnestly, "I do not believe women are inferior. But I do believe that people are more important than principles. I would be glad to help Mama with the housework but there is a very good reason why I can't."

"What is it?" Frances demanded.

Their mother came through the kitchen door, her arms around a large laundry basket, filled with steaming clothes. She dropped the basket near the kitchen window that opened to the outdoor washline. Later, when everybody was finished with breakfast, and out of the kitchen, she would hang out the laundry. For the moment, she sank into a chair, and took a deep breath.

"Why don't you ask Mama?" said Mr. Green.

"Would anybody like a few matzo-meal pancakes?" suggested Mrs. Green.

"All right, I will ask her," said Frances. "Mama, why doesn't Papa ever do any housework? You work all day without stopping, but even when he's home, and not doing anything, he doesn't help you. Why is that?"

"Papa do housework?" Mrs. Green was scandalized. "Why should Papa do housework?"

"Because it's only fair," Frances insisted. "There shouldn't be 'woman's work' or 'man's work.' Men and women should do the same work, and have the same rights and privileges. Actually, Mama, the best thing would be for you to go out to work."

"Go to work? Why should I go to work?"

"Because it's degrading for a woman to live off her husband, and work like a slave without wages."

"Your papa," said her mother, with unusual spirit, "works very hard to support his family. That's his work. When he comes home, it's not his job to help around the house. That's my job, and I can't stand to see a man in the kitchen. I have no respect at all for a woman who lets her husband help around the house."

Papa smiled at Frances, shrugged his shoulders helplessly, and picked up his newspaper.

Mama continued, "I only hope for you, Frances, that one day, you'll meet a nice, young man, who'll make a good living for you so you can stay home and take care of your family too."

"When I get married," said Frances emphatically, "I plan on working even if I have children, and my husband will share the housework with me, fifty-fifty."

"Just make sure you don't tell that to any boy you go out with," said her mother, "or you'll never get married."

"But I think Frances is right," Marv said slowly. "Why should a woman have to do housework if she doesn't want to? There's no reason why men shouldn't help in the house."

"So?" said Frances, "And what are you going to do about it?"

And what was he going to do about it? Mama didn't like anybody to help her. Betsy and Frances might be allowed to set the table and occasionally wash the dishes, but Marv, being a male, was never permitted to help around the house. So what *was* he going to do? Which brought him back to thinking about something beautiful and useful for Mama.

Was there something he could design that would simplify her "hand washing"? The only thing he could think of was attaching a set of paddles—he happened to have four ping-pong rackets downstairs—to an old fan motor—which could agitate the water in the bathtub, and move the clothes around.

On Monday his mother was ironing a mound of clothes. The iron sizzled as it rode over the dampened garments, and the air smelled steamy and sweet. There was an ink roller downstairs from a broken printing press. Marv wondered if he could rig it up to move back and forth across the ironing board. A hose attached to a tea kettle could direct steam at the clothes and a spring loaded foot pedal would activate the whole business.

Tuesday Mama was washing the bedroom windows. She was sitting out on the ledge, stretching up to the outermost corner of the raised window, and the glass caught the sunshine and held it. Perhaps it might be possible—yes, he was sure it could be made to work —to have two flat, paper hanger brushes attached and riding on vertical tracks on either side of the outside windows. A string could pull them up, and a spring could pull them down. Beneath, a soapy trough of water could be waiting.

Wednesday, there were papers spread over the kitchen and dining room floors. Mama had been down on her hands and knees washing and waxing the linoleum. He toyed with the idea of a two-headed mop, one head for washing and one for waxing, but could not build up any enthusiasm for it.

But on Thursday, when he spotted his mother, struggling up the front stairs, her face red, her breath coming hard, and two heavy packages in her arms,

Marv suddenly knew exactly what he could do with that hank of rope he had found the previous weekend, and how his problem of making something useful for his mother had been solved.

He spent Friday after school, constructing a frame around the top of one of the kitchen windows on the outside.

"Now what?" Frances questioned, opening the window when she arrived home from school.

Marv was kneeling on the top of the ladder. There were several nails in his mouth, and his eyes were on a wheel, or rather the rim of a wheel, that had once belonged to Estelle Abramson's baby carriage. The wheel had just been secured to the center of the frame right above the window.

"Now what?"

Marv took the nails out of his mouth, and smiled mysteriously into his sister's face. They were exactly level, she on the inside of the window, he on the outside.

"Shh, it's a surprise. For Mama."

Frances snorted. "Some surprise! You can hear you banging a mile away. Don't you think she knows you're here?"

"I guess so," Marv admitted, "but she doesn't know I'm making *her* something. She's used to hearing me but she doesn't know it has anything to do with her."

"What are you making?"

Marv shook his head playfully. "It's going to be a

surprise for everybody. But Frances, you're really going to like it, I can promise you that. And it's really going to be something useful, very useful, for Mama."

Marv chuckled. Frances watched her brother chuckling. She looked at the nails in his hand, and the hammer. She leaned out of the window, and looked up at the lop-sided frame with the wheel from the carriage that had once held the baby, Estelle Abramson.

"Marv," she said, "whatever it's going to be, it looks horrible. Did you do what I told you, Saturday? Did you go to the library?"

"Yes, Frances, I did." And he had, hadn't he? "And like you said, Frances, this time I'm making something that's really useful." Marv grinned. "Just wait, Frances. You'll be just crazy about this."

"I certainly hope so," Frances said doubtfully. She slammed the window, and Marv watched the back of her moving off. It wasn't easy working when people interrupted you. If there was an outdoor shade on a window as well as an indoor shade, then a person could work undisturbed. It wouldn't really be any trouble at all to put up an outside shade. He had the hardware, and even an old window shade roller. There was also a rubber sheet he'd picked up outside the Bronx Hospital, and perhaps if he cut it to size, and attached it to the roller.

Marv was halfway down the ladder when he remembered what he was supposed to be working on.

He scurried up the ladder again, spun the wheel, and estimated where the other wheel would have to go.

On Saturday, he completed the placement of ropes and pulleys. Sunday, his parents decided to visit Aunt Sadie and Uncle Lester. Betsy said she would go too. So far so good. He wanted to have the place to himself for the final installation. Frances said she had to stay home and study. Where? Marv held his breath. It was a chilly day, and Frances had a paper to write. His luck held. Frances would be working in her room.

There was an old medicine chest in the basement that was too narrow and the top of a stove with a hinged door that was too heavy. Out in the yard, over near the tree, Marv found an old pigeon coop, half-buried and nearly forgotten. Last year, he had tried unsuccessfully to train two pigeons—hi-jacked from the park—to be carrier pigeons. The pigeon coop was too fragile, but it reminded him of the rabbit cage he had built a year or so earlier. As he remembered, it had two doors of chicken wire and wood strips in the front. The cage, when it was finally excavated from the south-central mound, proved to be too shallow. Marv removed the doors, and attached them to the cleanest of his orange crates. They fit very well, and he opened up the other side of the crate, and made two other doors there as well. There remained less than a foot of space above the doors which meant that nothing was likely to fall out.

After that, everything ran smoothly. It was an unusually cold, cloudy day, and Frances remained in her room. Marv drilled a hole on the top of the box, and attached the rope. At last it was finished, and hung there ready and willing—a dumbwaiter to hoist his mother's heavy packages up, and to spare her the agony of carrying them herself.

He sat down on the ground, and looked up at it. Useful it certainly was, and perhaps, and he didn't want to brag about his own work, beautiful as well. He stood up, and patted the box. All set to go on her maiden voyage, she was, just asking to go. He filled a bag with coals from the cellar, arranged it on the inside of the box, closed the door, saluted, laughed, and began raising the box up toward the kitchen window. Steadily, smoothly, sleekly, the box rose. When the top of it reached the lower edge of the frame, it swayed gently, tilted forward, the doors opened, and Marv sprang out of the way as a shower of coals rained down from above. As soon as he let go of the rope, the box came whizzing down, hit the ground, and one of the doors flew off.

But the question that had been nagging him for months found a crystal clear answer. That ratchet movement in the clock—of course, now he saw the light! He could use a ratchet movement, like the one in the clock, to regulate, to slow down, to insure a slow and steady and safe rise and fall of the dumbwaiter, even if somebody did let go. Marv picked up the broken door and smiled at it.

"What happened?" Frances cried, leaning out the window. "Are you all right, Marv?"

"I'm fine, Frances. Don't worry. I just figured something important out."

"Well, how about figuring it out quietly for a change?"

The rest of the afternoon passed in glory. When his parents returned that evening Marv was waiting for them in front of the house.

"Mama, Papa, come with me." Marv's face and hands were filthy. There was coal dust on his hair, and all over his shirt, "Betsy, would you please go and ask Frances to come out. I want her to see this too."

He drew his parents down the cellar steps, through the basement, and up the stairs that led to the yard.

A strange, bulky object, attached to ropes and wheels, swayed in the cool wind, shrouded in old blankets and sheets.

Mrs. Green glanced at the mysterious object, and then looked solicitously at her son. "Marvin," she asked, "did you have lunch?"

"Sure, Mama," Marv said, excitement making his voice sound very high, "and Mama, just wait till you see what I made for you."

"For me?" said his mother. "Thank you very much, but Marvin, you're not wearing a sweater, and it's cold outside."

"A surprise?" said his father. "Isn't that nice? I wonder what it is."

Frances and Betsy came through the door, and Marv said, "Ladies and Gentlemen, but I really should say Lady because this is for you, Mama. From now on, no more dragging heavy bundles up the stairs, Mama. All that is a thing of the past. Now, Mama, when you come home from shopping with heavy bundles, you will have a faithful servant waiting to help you."

Betsy tittered, Papa smiled, and Marv pulled the sheets and blankets off the dumbwaiter. Nobody said anything. Marv lifted the bag of coals onto the box, and turning a handle, attached to a unique, double ratchet mechanism, began to raise it. Click-click-click-click went the sound of the dumbwaiter, and Marv demonstrated how the double ratchet handle regulated, with beautiful precision, the speed at which the box was raised. He pulled it up to the window, exactly where he wanted it, dropped the rope, smiled into the astonished faces of his family, and commented proudly, "No hands."

He hurried down the stairs of the basement, calling back over his shoulder, "Don't anybody move." He tore up the stairs to the kitchen and opened the window. There, he demonstrated how the groceries could be unloaded. The box would remain right outside the kitchen window until it was needed again. Maintenance would be no trouble either. He personally would keep the wheels oiled, and check the rope from time to time. He would just ask Mama and the girls too, whenever they used it, to keep it clean and to occasionally . . .

"Marv!"

Marv stopped talking. Questions? There were bound to be questions. How did he get the idea of making the dumbwaiter? The design? And above all, how did he know to make that double ratchet handle? He wanted to hear what his mother would say. Naturally, she'd be pleased. What a difference this would make in her life. He smiled at her, and she smiled back. But she didn't say anything. Frances did.

"Marv! You idiot! I give up. You just can't do anything right, can you? Didn't you realize that in order for Mama to use this hideous lift, she would have to carry her bundles down the cellar steps, through the cellar and over all your booby traps, up another flight of stairs into the yard? That's about twice as far as she'd have to go just carrying the bundles up the front steps." Frances hissed all her s's as she spoke, so she was pretty annoyed.

"Frances," Papa said soothingly, "it was very thoughtful of Marvin, and I'm sure Mama will be happy to have this. After all, he couldn't put it in the front. The living room window doesn't even open."

"Which is a very good reason," Frances said mercilessly, "for him to put another ugly, useless monstrosity in the back. As usual."

For the first time in a long time, Marv felt like crying. He was so sure this time, but no, he'd gone and flubbed it again.

Betsy and Papa made soft, sympathetic comments before they went up, and Mama said he should stay inside and have a sandwich. But he drifted down to the garden after the others had gone. His hand rested on the double ratchet handle. His fingers followed the outline of the teeth. They had been made out of two thick orange crate ends, lined with strips cut from a tin can. He was actually prouder of it than of anything he had ever made before. He had not even had a chance to show it to the others. It was possible some of them, maybe even Frances, didn't even know what a double ratchet was. But he did not think this was the time to show her.

Peter Wedemeyer moved across the street on June 23. It was the only good thing that happened in June. On June 9, Norway had fallen to the German Army. On June 22, France.

The cartoon in the paper showed a beautiful girl with long hair and a slim, delicate neck, lying on the ground weeping. Above her, a huge, black boot was poised to strike. Across the girl's skirt were the words *La Belle France,* and across the heel of the boot, the word GERMANY.

In three months, Hitler had invaded six countries. Only Great Britain remained now to fight on all by herself. In two months' time, Hitler promised his people, Great Britain too would lie at his feet.

Papa was unhappy. Most of his relatives lived in Poland, where he was born. Since the German invasion of Poland in 1939, there had been no word from them. Horrible, unbelievable stories were growing more and more persistent about the cruel treatment the Germans inflicted upon their captives, particularly if they were Jewish.

There was one cousin whom Papa loved the best. His name was Lebel, and he and Papa had grown up together, and been close friends when they were boys in Poland. Lebel had left Poland shortly after Papa, but had gone to France. He lived in a small town, and was also a baker. There had been a letter from him three months ago, with a picture enclosed. He and his wife and two daughters were standing on a country road. There were mountains behind them, and the older girl's hair was streaming in the wind. Both children were laughing.

"This Hitler is insane," cousin Lebel had written, "but we know it will only be a matter of a few months before he will be defeated. We are not afraid."

Papa was. He told stories about how he and Lebel had grown up together, how they had run away from home once and slept two nights in a barn with lots of mice for company. He told them how handsome Lebel was, how intelligent, and how close they always were

—"like brothers." He was afraid now for Lebel and his family.

Frances was upset too. She couldn't decide what the United States should do. Go to war? Stay out of it? Something had to be done, but what? The indecision made her temper more prickly than ever. She and Papa never seemed to talk about anything else. Papa was looking for a way to help the people he knew and loved escape. Frances wanted to change the world. They did not usually agree.

Peter Wedemeyer was sitting in the first seat, third row when school started on June 23. Mr. Henderson asked everybody in that row to move back one seat to make room for the new boy. He was unquestionably the smallest boy in the class, and turned out to be the youngest as well—just twelve. He had been skipped from 7B[1] in his old school to 8A[2] upon his entrance into P.S. 63. It was understood that he was only in the 2 class because he'd been skipped, and was one of those rare phenomena, seldom found in 2 classes—a smart kid.

He was all movement. His eyes moved. His nose twitched. His mouth was either opening or closing, and his hand was generally in the air. He knew all the answers, and Mr. Henderson's eyes, when they rested upon him, contained an unfamiliar tender glow.

He should have been the most unpopular kid in the class as well as the smallest, the youngest, and the smartest. But he was so good in punch ball, so quick a runner, so self-assured, and so friendly, that by the end of the day, everybody liked him. Maybe Veronica Ganz didn't like him. She was the biggest kid in the class, and the meanest. She didn't like anybody, and nobody much liked her. So you couldn't count Veronica Ganz.

The next morning, as Marv came down the front steps of his house, he saw Peter coming down the steps of his, across the street. Peter lived in the newest apartment house on the street. It had awnings over the windows in the summertime, and the janitor polished all the brass around the doors. There was even a mural painted in the outer vestibule.

Marv saw Peter first. He hesitated, not knowing whether to wave, call or just walk on. No decision on his part was necessary because as soon as Peter spotted Marv he waved, called, "Hiya, Marv," and crossed the street without any hesitation at all.

They walked to school, picking up Bill Stover, Ralph Crespi and Paul Lucas. The conversation turned to baseball, and Peter stated decisively that the Yankees would definitely win the series that year. He told them that Dizzy Dean was all washed up as a pitcher, and that Joe DiMaggio was the greatest outfielder that ever lived. He had an opinion about everything. Germany would be beaten by England in February 1941; the earth would disintegrate as a living planet in two million years when the sun burned itself out; and the cure for leprosy would be announced any day now.

That afternoon, he walked home with Marv. They ended up in front of Peter's house and Marv hesitated.

"You live in that little house?" Peter asked wistfully. "All my life I've only lived in apartment houses. I always wanted to live in my own house."

"No kidding?" Marv was surprised. He thought most people preferred living in apartment houses, particularly if they had elevators.

"What are you doing today?" asked Peter, his eyes still on Marv's house.

"Just poking around in the garden, I guess. Nothing special."

"You've got your own garden?" Peter's eyes were wide. "I guess I'll come along with you. Come on in my house, and I'll tell my mother."

They entered the vestibule, and Marv had a few seconds to inspect the magnificent mural painted over the letter boxes while Peter rang the bell. The mural depicted a huge lake, running around the perimeter of the hall. It was sunrise, and a brilliant orange sun tipped the tops of the trees surrounding the lake in bright points of yellow, pink, red, and orange. The waters reflected the sun's magnificence with triangular splashes of more red, pink, orange and yellow. In the midst of all this radiance, one small boat, right above the left hand mailboxes greeted the dawn. Two tiny dark figures were in the boat, but it was impossible to make out what they were doing.

"Z–z–z–z–z," sounded the buzzer.

Peter opened the hall door, and beckoned for Marv to come. A woman was standing in front of the apartment door marked 3A.

"Peter," she said, and she smiled and kissed him. She looked as if she was going to kiss him again, but Peter moved back slightly, and said quickly, "Mama, this is Marv Green. He's in my class, and he lives across the street."

"How do you do," said Mrs. Wedemeyer. "Come in, Marv." She smiled, and patted his shoulder as he went by. She invited him to join Peter in a glass of milk and some cookies, and sat and talked to them while they were eating. She asked him how many times he had been on the honor roll, and if he had ever skipped. He answered "Never" to both. Then she told him that Peter had skipped twice, and that he had been on the honor roll for every term he'd been in school. She told him that Peter had said his first word at five months. It was "Gooboo," which meant garbage.

Peter jumped up, and said, "Come on, Marv, I'll put my books away, and then we can go."

He followed Peter into his room, a very neat room that made Marv feel like tiptoeing.

On the way out, Mrs. Wedemeyer said, "Come home

by five, Peter. It was very nice meeting you, Marv."
She smiled, and patted his shoulder going out just as
she had coming in. She was a very nice lady, he supposed.

Frances was having some milk and cookies at the
kitchen table, and his mother was peeling potatoes.

"Mama, Frances, this is Peter Wedemeyer. He's a
new boy in my class, and he lives across the street."

Frances nodded.

"Very pleased to meet you," said Mama. "Come, sit
down, boys, and have some milk and cookies."

"We did already at Peter's house," said Marv, but
his mother was pouring the milk so they sat down,
and had some more milk and cookies.

His mother asked Peter when they had moved in.
She said· moving was such a nightmare, and he
should be sure to tell his mother that if she needed
anything, anything at all, she should please call Ida
Green right away.

Frances joined the conversation.

"How old are you?" she asked Peter.

"Twelve."

"And you're in Marv's class? How come?"

"I skipped."

Frances looked significantly at Marv.

"I suppose you read a lot."

"I sure do."

"What kind of books do you read?"

"Stamps. I save stamps. Snakes. Natural history.

Astronomy. Archaeology. Electronics, and . . . poetry."

Frances offered Peter another cookie. They chatted awhile, and it was plain to see that Peter was making quite an impression on Frances. She never spoke to Ralph or Frank when they came over, and they certainly never went out of their way to start a conversation with her. She scared them. She scared lots of people.

But Peter was fearless. He laughed, and spoke without hesitation on any subject she brought up. Every so often Frances shot an angry glance in Marv's direction. He knew she was comparing them, unfavorably for him, and he could hardly blame her. He was enjoying Peter too, enjoying his bright, quick voice, and the pleasant excitement he seemed to generate.

Up in Marv's room, Peter turned nearly speechless. For a while, the only things he said were "What's this?" or "What's that?" as he moved from one object to another.

"Do you want to see the garden?" Marv suggested, pointing to the window.

Peter looked. "Where is it?"

"Down there."

Peter looked again. "It doesn't look like a garden. Where are the flowers?"

"It's not that kind of a garden."

They went down into it, and for a little while, Peter

114

resumed "What's this?" and "What's that?" as he moved from mound to mound. He tried the revolving doors, and sent some bricks up on the dumbwaiter. Marv still hadn't taken it down. His mother, whenever she was around and she remembered, made a special effort to send her bundles aloft. But he knew she was being kind, and if anything, the dumbwaiter made things harder for her. He would take it down one of these days but he couldn't bear to think of that double ratchet handle lying somewhere forgotten.

So for the past few weeks, he was back to working normally. A bonanza of bricks from a torn down movie house lay all over the garden. Marv had drawn a circle about five feet in diameter, and had laid the first three circular rows of bricks in what was to become a brick igloo.

Peter inspected the site with a knowledgeable eye. He began talking. "In the old school, I made a desk set, and a tie rack, and it was a snap. I even took a book out of the library, and made a candy dish from the instructions. Here, let me give you a hand. Maybe I can suggest a couple of a new ideas."

But Peter didn't know how to mix cement, and Marv showed him. He also didn't understand that the bricks couldn't be set squarely over each other. Marv showed him that too. He also showed him how to angle the bricks toward the center so that each row grew smaller as the igloo shape began to emerge.

Two-thirds of the way up, they ran out of bricks.

"We can build a chicken wire frame, and cement it the rest of the way up," said Marv.

"When?" Peter's voice was eager. He laid down his trowel, crawled through the opening in the igloo, and stood up inside.

"Tomorrow?" Marv questioned. He hoped Peter would come. It had been fun working with him although in general, he preferred working by himself.

"Great," said Peter. "I'm going to look up igloos in my encyclopedia, and see if it doesn't give some dimensions for the dome."

Marv nodded gratefully.

At supper that night, Frances said, "That's quite a boy you brought home today."

"He sure is," Marv agreed.

"I'm glad to see you can make friends with someone who has a head on his shoulders for a change."

Marv was silent.

"All Marv's friends are nice boys," Mama said.

"Yes, but this boy is intelligent. He reads and thinks. It's about time Marv had a friend who could show him that there are other things in this world besides banging and making messes."

"You know who I like?" said Betsy. "That nice-looking boy, Ralph. He's so polite, and so is his brother, Alan. He's in my class, and the other day he picked up my notebook when I dropped it in the hall, and he walked with me to algebra, and held the door open for me."

"Are you finished?" Frances inquired. She turned back to Marv. "What did you do today with Peter? What did you talk about?"

"Nothing much."

"What?"

"Well, I showed him my room."

"And then?"

"We went out to the garden."

"Yes?"

"We just fooled around. Nothing special."

"You mean that bright, intelligent boy just potted around with you in the back."

"I guess so."

"What were you doing?"

"Frances, pass me some Greek salad please."

"What were you doing?"

"We were making something."

"What?"

"An igloo."

Papa began talking about Harry Rosen's cousin in Holland who had managed to get out of the country after the Nazis invaded it. Harry had a friend who worked at the Red Cross, and Papa planned on going to see him to find out if there was any way of getting Lebel and his family out of France.

Mama said she hoped it would do some good, and that Papa shouldn't worry. Lots of people were escaping from Hitler, and maybe Lebel had managed to go with his family to Switzerland.

"Will it never end?" Frances cried. "All this sense-less killing and fighting?"

Betsy got up and began to clear the table. Mama said gently, "Let's talk about something cheerful."

"Yes," said Frances, "wouldn't it be lovely to live in a world where the conversations only dealt with the cheerful and the beautiful."

Papa sighed, and nodded in agreement. He stood up. "Maybe I'll write to that man at the Red Cross before I go to work."

Mama moved off toward the sink, and began washing the dishes.

Frances seemed deep in her own thoughts. Carefully Marv began rising from his chair. But she saw him, or at least she saw one person who still remained to listen.

"Why should people destroy when they can build? Why should they kill when they can save? This is such a beautiful world, and man should be a force for good instead of evil. One of these days, the world will be a different place, and people will commit themselves to working for the good of all mankind. Then there won't be any reason for war."

How beautifully she spoke! How right she was! How right she always was! Every single bone in his body agreed with her. "You're right. Yes, you're right," he cried.

Her eyes focused on him. As soon as she saw it was Marv, she said witheringly, "You! Some worker for the good of anybody you'd be! You're a corrupter, that's what you are. You put guns into people's hands, and now, you bring home a sensible, intelligent boy, and teach him to make igloos—igloos in the Bronx, in the middle of June!"

Why was it she never allowed him to agree with her, when he agreed with her so absolutely? What would it take to make her approve of him? Even before the drums began beating, Marv was swearing, deep inside himself, to try again. And this time for sure, he would make something so beautiful and so useful that Frances would have to approve.

10

They finished the igloo before school was out, and Peter said they should have a party to celebrate, the way the Eskimos did. Ralph and Frank came, and so did Bill Stover and Paul Lucas. The completed dimensions of the igloo were five feet in diameter by three feet high, which gave them plenty of room to lean all over one another while they ate.

Peter said whale blubber and the undigested contents of a caribou's stomach were the usual refreshments at Eskimo parties. But everybody agreed since the above mentioned were hard to find that chocolate bars, marshmallows, and gum drops could be substituted.

After the eating was completed, they huddled inside the igloo, and discussed their plans for the summer.

Peter's family had taken "a room" at Rockaway Beach. He would swim every day, and spend every night on the boardwalk playing skee ball, and eating frozen custards. None of the other boys had ever spent a summer at Rockaway Beach, and they drank in the details of Peter's previous vacations there with great interest and disguised envy.

"It's boring doing nothing but swim every day," said Frank. He told them he was going away for four weeks to a camp that his church sponsored. There would be hikes, overnites, campfires, crafts and swimming too, and in a lake which was more fun than ocean swimming.

Peter said he wished he could go to camp too, but his mother still acted like he was five.

"Mine too," said Paul. "She makes me drink four glasses of milk a day, and I hate milk."

For a while the conversation ranged over the different methods of maternal tortures, and then returned to the summer curriculum.

"I'll be going with my mother and brother to visit my grandmother in South Bend," said Bill.

"Where's that? New Jersey?" asked Ralph.

"No, stupid, Indiana."

"I didn't know you had a grandmother in Indiana," Ralph said respectfully. "I never met anybody from Indiana. What's it like in Indiana?"

"Hot, and you eat ices and go swimming."

Ralph was disappointed. "It sounds like the Bronx. But at least it's someplace. I never get to go anywhere. I'll be around the whole summer."

Ralph's father owned a hardware store, and his mother worked there nearly every day. Ralph and his brother, Alan, had to help with the shopping and cleaning. Everybody said the store made a lot of money, but the two boys never seemed to go anyplace interesting.

Paul said, "We're not going anyplace either. Maybe you and I can do something together, Ralph."

"Like what?"

"Swim in Crotona Park?"

"OK."

"The Y has outings every Monday for boys nine to fourteen. Are you a member?"

"No. Are you?"

"Yes, and I can bring a friend."

"Gee, that's great. And listen. Paul, my uncle rents rowboats over in City Island."

"My mother would never let me go."

"But my brother can take us. He's fifteen, and you can wear a life preserver, and my uncle will lend us fishing poles."

Once begun, the possibilities of good times in the

city seemed endless. The three boys who were going away began to feel cheated.

"And Marv will be around too," said Ralph, searching in the gloom of the igloo's interior. "Marv!"

"Uh?"

"You're going to be around too, aren't you? The three of us can have a great time."

Marv had been staring at one of the dimly lit brick walls inside the igloo. As his friends talked, he had been thinking of an array of future useful and beautiful projects, and watching them take shape against the wall's darkness. The fishing poles mentioned by Ralph had been projected on the wall, and he had lingered over the ratchet in the handle. It reminded him of his double ratchet in the dumbwaiter which still hung outside the kitchen window.

Why not remove the whole thing, and hang the handle outside the living room window? The window did not open because the frame had warped many years ago, after a hurricane. He could fix the window —that in itself would be good. But then he could attach a mailbox to a chain which moved around the double ratchet handle just outside the window. Every morning, the postman could deposit the mail in the box and . . . wait . . . he could even arrange for a buzzer to sound inside. Nothing to it. He would simply install a soft metal contact inside the mailbox. The weight of just one letter falling on it would turn it on, and start a buzzer sounding. Then the family would

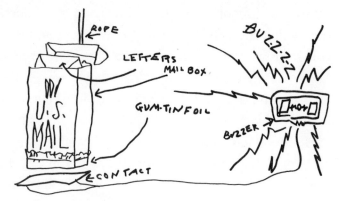

know for sure that the mail had arrived. There would be no guesswork. Once the buzzer sounded, somebody could come to the window, open it, turn the handle, and draw in the mail. It would save them all the trouble of going outside. Even if you only had to open the door, and reach out, you might check several times before the mail actually came. With his plan, all uncertainty would be gone forever.

"You're going to be around, too, aren't you? The three of us can have a great time."

"Sure," Marv said confidently. Once he put up the mailbox, and fixed the window, he would have the whole summer free to swim, fish, row or take care of his own affairs.

Peter left the next day. Marv spent the morning at his house. Peter said he wouldn't be just swimming and playing on the boardwalk. He planned on reading some chemistry books which Frances had suggested. He also intended to start a shell collection and had borrowed a book from the library on shell identification which he could keep for the whole summer. Peter's voice grew higher as the time to go approached. Marv watched the family load boxes of dishes and linens, suitcases and bags of food into Peter's Uncle Jake's truck.

He stood on Peter's stoop, and watched the family pile into the truck. Perhaps they might ask him to come and visit one day. It took only about two hours to get out to Rockaway. He edged a little closer to the front of the stoop to be plainly in sight.

Peter and his father sat in the open back of the truck with the boxes and luggage while Peter's mother and older sister, Rosalie, sat in the front with his Uncle Jake.

The car started to move. "Goodbye, goodbye, Marv," Peter shouted. "I'll see you after the summer." He shouted something else too, but Marv couldn't hear what it was.

He stepped out into the street, looking after the truck, and hoping it would stop. But it did not. Peter's hand was still waving as the truck turned the corner.

The next day, Marv took down the dumbwaiter. He separated all the parts and began hunting around for a chain and a reasonable facsimile of a mailbox. His enthusiasm was not up to its usual pitch so when his father reminded him at lunchtime that the Bakers Union, Local 27 was holding its summer picnic at

Tibbetts Brook the next day, and that each child could bring a friend, Marv was pleased to put aside his work for the time being.

He would bring a friend, and with Peter away, his choice fell upon Ralph. Nobody answered the doorbell at Ralph's house, but as he started back, he met both Ralph and his brother, Alan, walking along the street. Ralph said sure he could come.

"You don't have to bring anything to eat," Marv said. "The union takes care of that. But don't forget your bathing suit, and a towel because there's a pool there, and be at my house by ten."

"How many kids can you invite?" Alan asked.

"Only one. Gee, I'm sorry, Alan, I wish I could invite you too."

"That's OK. Don't worry about it."

"Where are you going now?" Ralph asked.

"No place special."

"Do you want to play handball?"

"OK."

"Let's go to my house, and get a ball."

Alan walked along with them. He asked a lot of questions about what Marv's parents were doing that summer. What was Frances doing? Where was she right now? And wasn't there somebody else? Oh yes —Betsy—and what was she doing, and where was she now?

He seemed very interested to learn that Frances was at the library, and not very interested to hear that

Betsy was last seen heading toward Goldberg's Yarn Store on Bathgate Avenue to buy some wool for a sweater.

"I'll see you fellows later," he said, when they reached his house.

"Aren't you coming with us?" Ralph asked.

"No, I've got to meet a friend."

"Since when? You said before you didn't have anything doing today."

"I forgot," Alan said, hurrying off.

At supper that night, Mama said she hoped it wouldn't rain tomorrow as it had last year.

"I'm glad it's going to be at Tibbetts Brook this year," Frances said agreeably. "It's so pretty there, like the country almost."

"Did you children invite anybody?" Papa asked. "There will be plenty of food, and wait until you see the cake! Milton Wishingrad baked it, and when I say it's a work of art, I mean it's a work of art."

"Ralph's coming," Marv said.

Betsy laughed. Her eyes were very bright. "I was going to ask Helen Farber but on the way back from Goldberg's I met Alan Crespi. He walked me back, and I guess he must have heard Ralph talk about the picnic, and he was so interested, and said how he wished he could go to a picnic like that, so—I asked him, and he's coming too."

"Maybe there's another brother for Frances to invite," Mama laughed.

But Frances was offended. She stood up, and pushed her chair back. "You don't have to find someone for me to invite," she said angrily. "If I wanted to invite somebody, it would be somebody intelligent, and I don't feel like inviting anybody tomorrow."

"What did I say?" Mama said, in answer to the three pairs of reproachful eyes which fastened on her after Frances left.

It did not rain the next day. Alan and Ralph arrived at 9:15, and were persuaded to have another breakfast. They took the train to Van Cortlandt Park, and walked up the trail that led to Tibbetts Brook.

As Frances had said, it was like being in the country. The path was edged by trees and green fields. There was not one single trace of a house, a street car, or anything that means city. Other members of the union, their families and friends converged on the path, and there was talk, laughter and children scampering over everybody's feet.

The older people began to sing first. They sang Jewish songs: *Rozhinkes Mit Mandlen, Lomir Zich Ibberbeten,* and the beautiful riddle song, *Tumbalalaika.*

> *Maydl, Maydl, ch'vill by dir fregen*
> *Vos ken vaksen, vaksen on regen?*
> *Vos ken brennen un nit oifheren?*
> *Vos ken beynken, vainen on treren?*
>
> *Narisher bocher vos dorftstu fregen*

A shtain ken vaksen, vaksen on regen
A libbe ken brennen un nit oifheren
*A hartz ken beynken, vainen on trerer.**

*Maiden, Maiden, I will ask you three questions
What can grow and grow without rain?
What can burn and not be consumed?
What can break without crying or tears?

Foolish boy, why must you ask
A stone can grow and grow without rain
Love can burn and not be consumed
A heart can break without crying or tears.

The younger people sang *Home on the Range, Clementine,* and some of them sang songs from the Spanish Civil War in 1936. They were such brave, stirring songs. The people who sang them then must have thought they were going to win. It gave Marv a hurt feeling in his stomach when the singers, now, on the path to Tibbetts Brook, shouted:

"But at Madrid
They shall not pass."

Because they had passed. It was four years ago but he could still remember how Frances had cried when Franco won the war. He turned to look at her, but she was nowhere among the doubles and triples of people who walked and sang together along the path. He spotted her finally, up ahead, walking by herself and not singing.

130

The food had arrived before they had. There was the most enticing array of sandwiches to await any hungry group of hikers—tongue sandwiches, roast beef, corned beef, egg salad, salami. The cake was truly a masterpiece—three tiered, covered with pink and white roses, and on the very top, stood a figure of a baker, holding a miniature cake like the one he was standing on. It tasted as good as it looked, and the root beer was ice cold.

In the pool, Alan demonstrated his swimming prowess by dragging Betsy, screaming into the pool, ducking her, swimming under her legs, and tossing her off his shoulders. Marv dived off the lowest diving board, and once off the highest. He held out his arms in front of him, his body taut, and tried to keep his legs together and his head down. His belly hit the water first, and he decided to go back to the lowest diving board.

He was on his way toward it when he met Frances. "Isn't this great?" he said.

Frances didn't answer. She kept going.

"Wait a minute," Marv called after her. He hurried up to her anxiously. "Where are you going? What's wrong?"

"Nothing's wrong. I've had enough swimming. I'm getting dressed. Maybe I'll take a walk."

She was looking over his shoulder as she spoke, and he turned and saw Betsy in the pool, laughing and screaming as both Ralph and Alan tugged and pushed at her.

"Boneheads!" Frances said savagely.

Marv looked at her face. It was tight and unhappy. It gave him the same hurt feeling inside that thinking about the Spanish Civil War had caused earlier that day.

"Hey, I'll come with you, Frances. I'm finished swimming."

"Why?" she asked. "You don't have to come. I didn't ask you."

"I know you didn't," he said carefully, "but I'm getting cold. I'll just tell Ralph, and then I'll get dressed, and meet you outside." He hurried off without looking at her. He felt embarrassed at seeing what was on her face.

They walked through the park, and found a little road that led deep into the trees. It must have been a private road because after they had walked on it for a while, they came to a small neat, very white house. There were flowers edging the building and the gravel path that led to the stairs. A small stream ran in front of the house, and a graceful arched foot bridge made of stone, spanned it. There was a white marble bird bath on the lawn, and a black, iron rooster weather vane on the pointed roof.

"How beautiful it is," said Frances. "Just imagine living in a place like this!"

Marv examined the house. It was a small house.

There wasn't anything better about this house than their own in the Bronx. A little paint, a few repairs, and their house would look just as good. All right, the setting was nicer here with all those trees and greenery.

"Frances, would you like to live in a house like this?" he asked.

"Would I!"

She began walking back up the path, and Marv took one more look before he followed her. The trees and the greenery *were* very nice, but he did not see how he could manage them. What he could manage though were the stream, the bridge, the bird bath and the weather vane. His heart began beating faster as the moment of decision hovered over him. He'd forget about the mailbox. It wasn't worthy anyway either as an appendage to his splendid double ratchet handle or as an offering to Frances.

"Are you coming? Or are you going to spend all night down there?"

"Uh—oh—sure—yeah—I'm coming."

He darted up the path. He didn't have to look back to see it all—the stream, the bridge, the bird bath and the weather vane—transported to the Bronx. And moving over the bridge, with a look on her face that would not embarrass him was Frances. He knew now for sure what the beautiful and useful project would be.

11

The weather vane was easy once he accepted his inability to draw a proper rooster like the one he saw on the weather vane at Tibbetts Brook. He knew how to draw fish so his weather vane would have a fish on top. As a matter of fact, it would have a whale. Marv found it easy drawing whales, and for several days, devoted his time to just that. He drew swimming whales, spouting whales, schools of whales, whales fighting sharks, harpooned whales, whales by moonlight and families of whales.

One day he drew a whale that made him suck his breath in. He had never drawn such a perfect whale—

cleanly shaped, blunt of nose, graceful of tail, and with such a friendly look on its face.

Unfortunately it was a small whale, and he figured that he needed one at least fifteen to eighteen inches long. Very carefully, he tried to copy it on to the side of an orange crate he had waiting. It was necessary to erase, and start over several times, but finally he had a drawing of the whale on the wood that he could look at with pride. He cut it out with a coping saw, sanded the edges, making sure to sand down the front sides of the whale's head so that it would be thinner than the back, and would face into the wind.

From his large collection of paint cans with varying amounts of paint, he selected a bright shade of orange for the whale's body and a deep purple for the eye. He painted it on both sides, and put it up to dry between the legs of a clothespin, propped in a bottle. Marv stood back, and inspected it. Very nice, very very nice, and yet, perhaps just a touch of color here and there might improve it even more. He had a large can of Kelly Green paint, and a small can of Inca Turquoise. He used the Kelly Green for the whale's belly and the Inca Turquoise for the fins. The effect was unbelievable. Never in his whole life, had he, ever for one moment, thought of himself as a person who possessed even a scrap of artistic talent, and yet, the magnificent whale stood there as a testament.

A few days later when it dried, Marv attached the whale to a ⅜" rod, about 18" long, and then sank that into a ⅜" piece of galvanized pipe—both excavated from the northernmost mound in the garden. Out of two black coat hangers, he made the directional bars with E, W, N, and S at the ends.

Then he had to wait. That was the hardest part of all. Frances would not be leaving until July fourteenth, which gave him four days with absolutely nothing to do.

Frances was going away for a month to pick fruit in a large orchard near Lake Erie. An article, in one of the magazines Frances read, told of a summer project being organized by Mr. Frank Davidson, an instructor at Columbia University. He wrote of the terrible poverty existing in the United States, and spoke particularly of the migratory workers who never knew from day to day where their next meal was coming from. In an attempt to let others know "how the other half lives" and "to develop understanding and compassion in the leaders of tomorrow," he and his wife and two teen-aged daughters were inviting a small group of college students, no more than twenty, to join them in spending a month living like migratory workers. They would work all day in the orchard, picking fruit, be paid the same wages and attempt to eat the same food and use the same facilities the other workers did. The college students would, however, be housed in separate buildings although they would have no additional comforts. The author would supervise all the boy students and sleep in the same building with them, while his wife did the same for the girl students. Applications from interested, able-bodied students were invited.

Frances applied, and received a letter which invited her to come for an interview at Mr. Davidson's house with "one of your parents."

"But why?" Mama cried, when Frances told of her summer plans. "You could work in a nice, clean office like Marian Hoffman's daughter, or even sell things in a department store. Why should you pick fruit?"

"Because I want to see what it's like. It's not right for me to *think* I know what it's like being poor. If I'm ever going to help people, I have to *know* what it's like."

"I'll tell you what it's like," Mama said. "It's miserable. That's what it's like."

Papa went with Frances. Mr. Davidson told them and the other students and parents who were there that he had done the same thing the previous summer. A healthy, clean-looking girl spoke about her experiences and how much she learned. They showed a moving picture of college students and migratory workers picking fruit together, sitting in front of shacks, and carrying sacks of fruit. Frances and the other students asked questions about what do you talk about to migratory workers, and how to prepare for being one. They were interested in equipment and farm machinery. Papa and most of the other parents wanted to know about sanitary conditions, medical facilities, and whether or not eating the same food as migratory workers, even for a period of a month, might not be harmful. Mr. Davidson was able to answer everybody's questions satisfactorily. Papa had no choice but to give his consent, and Frances was accepted as one of the twenty.

Mama was not satisfied. She kept saying "Why?" over and over again, which was strong for Mama. July fourteenth, a big truck full of students, and driven by Mr. Davidson stopped in front of their house and honked. Frances, in overalls, a bandanna on her head, a small suitcase in her hand, and a nervous look on her face, said goodbye to all of them.

"Why?" said Mama to Papa after she was gone. "Why does she have to be so different from everybody else?"

"I don't know," said Papa, "but I think it's probably because she's so much more intelligent than everybody else."

"Who needs it!" said Mama "She should only be happy, and she doesn't have to be so intelligent."

Papa said it was important to handle brilliant people right, and not always be standing in their way. He said he hoped Frances would not feel her family ever stood in her way in the important things, and then he began talking about Lebel. He said Lebel had been a brilliant boy, and had wanted to be a doctor. But his

140

father had not been sympathetic, so poor Lebel became a baker, and had to struggle all his life just like everybody else. But if he had been a doctor, he might have been rich, and he could have paid to get out of France when Hitler came in. Papa said he hoped he would never stand in his children's way of improving themselves the way Lebel's father had. Then he began to cry. There had been no word from Lebel, and nobody seemed able to know how to help.

Later in the day, everybody began to feel better. Naturally, they missed Frances, but Mama was singing, Betsy invited two of her girl friends up, and they were listening to songs on the radio and dancing. Papa went to a meeting, and Marv decided to put up his weather vane.

There was a slight pitch to the front of the roof, but Marv anchored his legs securely around the peak as he leaned over the roof, and began to nail a block of wood to the building. That done, he began securing the weather vane to the block.

The tops of people going by, the tops of garbage cans, light posts, and parked automobiles spread out below him like a map. The top of his mother came down the top of the steps, carrying a bag of garbage. The top of it contained carrot peelings and chicken bones.

"Hi, Ma," he shouted.

His mother looked up, and dropped the bag. Now he could see what lay below the top level of the garbage—paper wrappers, four corn cobs, some shreds of gray/green unidentifiable objects, and one broken cup.

"Marvin," his mother screamed, "don't fall!"

Marv put out one hand to steady himself. "Don't worry, I'm fine," he laughed. "How's the weather down there?"

"Marvin," yelled his mother. "Come right down, Marvin!"

"I will, Mama. I'm just putting this in place." He hammered the last nail in place, and moved himself back on the roof as the weather vane began spinning. How smoothly it went. Without any effort at all, it turned around and around and around and around. So did his head as he followed its motion around and around and around and around. Soon everything around him was spinning, and he closed his eyes and held on very tightly. When he opened his eyes, the weather vane had stopped. The whale's nose pointed south—no—southwest.

"Mama," he shouted, "there's a southwest wind blowing."

"Isn't that wonderful! Marvin, darling, please—come down, right now!"

He helped his mother pick up all the garbage, and promised never to work on the roof again. Three times she made him promise.

"I'm going to be working in the front on something for Frances," he assured his mother, and began explaining about the stream, the bridge, and the bird bath.

"I don't care," she interrupted, "what you do as long as it isn't on the roof."

Betsy and Papa also admired the weather vane, and both made him promise several more times never to do anything on the roof again.

The next day, he made the bird bath. His mother had once given him a blue and white speckled enamel basin she used to soak her feet in. It had chips on the edge and one large black spot on the side. Since he planned on painting it anyway, the chips and spot didn't matter. Otherwise it was in fine shape, and could hold plenty of birds.

It was times like this that you really congratulated yourself for not throwing out things others considered junk. He retrieved a twisted bicycle wheel without a tire from the coal bin, and dusted it off tenderly. The metal axle from the inside of an old carriage fitted neatly into the opening of the wheel. The bearings worked perfectly, and the wheel spun around easily if somewhat askew. He hammered the wheel straight before setting the basin in the center. He had no idea whether or not anybody else had ever thought up a revolving bird bath but he thought probably not. The thrill of being the first was only shaken by the question why.

Why?

Yes, why?

Why a revolving bird bath?

Yes.

Well, maybe birds like to be rocked when they take a bath?

No, they do not.

It makes them feel as if they're still in motion? Come on!

I know—animals.

What animals? Queenie? She's fourteen, and doesn't even have any teeth. Besides, she never went after birds.

Cat. That's what—cats.

Mmmm.

Bells. He had bells. At least fifty of those little silver bells found outside of Dale's Tap Dancing Studio when it went out of business. He could hang bells from each spoke, have strings going around the rim of the wheels and through the living room window. Say you were in the house, and saw some birds innocently bathing while some killer cats were stalking them. You would simply pull the strings, start the wheel moving, the bells jingling, and the cats would be scared off.

The proud knowledge of being the first to design a cat-free, revolving bird bath hit him again. After he had acknowledged the applause of birdlovers all over the world, he went to work.

Putting all the parts together presented no problem at all. But where would it go? He needed to decide

144

where the stream would run, and then he could decide about the bird bath.

He walked up and down the front stairs a couple of times, and then he backed away from the front of the house and considered it. To the right of the staircase was a small plot of crab grass with a clearing in the center. Frances had once planted some iris bulbs there, and last spring two or three of them had managed to make it up. Now then, if he ran the stream across the front of his house, including the staircase and the grassy plot, the stream would be roughly twenty feet long. Sadly, he had to acknowledge that such a stream would be just too costly. He simply did not have that much cement, and could not afford to buy it. But if he confined the stream to the front of the grassy plot, it would run, say ten feet long, and would easily be within the realm of financial possibility.

Marv stepped back further on the sidewalk, and squinted at what was now and what was yet to be. A bright, glittering stream ran the width of the lawn. A handsome, arched bridge spanned it onto a bright green patch of lawn in the center of which bloomed a group of jaunty iris. Smack in the middle of the iris, rose the bird bath.

Nothing remained but the work. He hurried to begin.

12

Not counting the drifters, by the end of the first week, there were six steady workers who showed up each morning eager for work. They included Paul, Ralph, Roslyn Kaufman, Stanford Jackson, Lucy Allen and her brother, Seymour. Their good nature and eagerness for hard work made Marv feel even more strongly than ever how lucky he was, ordinarily, to have a place in the back to work where nobody could see him. It was seldom there that he was faced with this problem of man-power.

Roslyn Kaufman was the least trouble of all. Roslyn was three and a half. She brought her pail and shovel every day, and while the others dug out the trench, she made rows of mud pies along the banks. It was only that she took the mud pies so seriously, and cried so hard if anybody stepped on one. Roslyn's mother generally brought a folding chair outside, and sat in front of Marv's house where she could keep an eye on her daughter.

Stanford Jackson's mother never seemed to have a chance to sit. Besides Stanford, who was four, she had twin baby girls, and was forever pushing them in their double baby carriage. The babies cried all the time, and must have required a tremendous supply of food because Mrs. Jackson spent a lot of time shopping.

"Marvin," she would say, "would you mind keeping an eye on Stanford while I'm at the market. I won't be gone long."

Stanford wasn't too much trouble although he loved to slide down the piles of earth as the crew dug out the trench. Whenever he caused a landslide, and somebody yelled at him, his big, dark eyes would look so mournful that it was hard to stay angry.

After a while, Stanford and Roslyn found their way out to the garden, and spent part of their time playing back there. Roslyn's mother had to move her chair along with them, but she didn't seem to mind. Neither did the rest of the crew.

Marv had always admired Paul's sense of humor, but it was hard concentrating on mixing cement or remembering measurements when somebody kept

cracking jokes all the time. He was usually glad to see Ralph, and it was certainly true that Ralph worked much faster than anybody else. He also hurt himself more than anybody else. By the end of a couple of weeks, Ralph was covered with bandages and adhesive tape. He had also required a stitch in the tongue—it was still not completely clear how he got his tongue cut on the wheel of the bird bath while it was revolving —and had fallen into the trench several times while the cement was drying. Of course, once painted, the blood stains would disappear. Nevertheless, Marv was always encouraging when Ralph and Paul considered taking some time off to go swimming or boating.

But Lucy Allen, aged nine, and her brother, Seymour, aged seven, were the most trouble of all. They were completely tireless, devoted, and spent almost every moment of every day at the construction site. They could not be discouraged. They pleaded for work, and would do anything except go on the errands to faraway places that Marv tried to plan daily for them.

Frances was to be gone for a month. Originally, Marv expected to be finished in one week but because of the help he was receiving, by the end of the third week, he was still not through. He abandoned his original idea for an arched bridge over the stream, and built a cement slab bridge on three wooden planks. No sooner had he poured the cement than a swarm of kids, including his steadies, spread them-

149

selves over the drying cement and began decorating it. The finished bridge was embellished with borders of marbles, flowers made of Coca-Cola bottle tops with pebble stems and leaves, handprints, footprints, scallops of shells and bits and pieces of broken flower pots, crockery, bubble gum, keys, and buttons.

It was not exactly as he had planned, but at least it was finished. So was the bird bath. He was sorry he had allowed Lucy and Seymour to do the landscaping around it. Lucy thought the crab grass looked awful, and had insisted upon making it prettier. She and Seymour pulled up all the crab grass, and planted seeds. But the work crew kept stepping all over them, and nothing grew except for an uneven stubble of more crab grass.

With four days to go before Frances' return, the cement in the trench still needed to be painted before it could be filled with water. It had been drying for a week, and Marv ran a worried hand up and down and all around the inside of the trench.

"I guess it's dry," he told Ralph.

"What color are you going to paint it?"

"I don't have enough paint to paint it one color," Marv said. "I could pour a few cans together, but I always get brown when I do that, except it's not really brown either, and whatever it is, it's not pretty."

"If you mix blue and yellow together, you get green," Ralph reflected wisely, "and red and blue, you get purple, and red and yellow, you get orange."

"I know what you're supposed to get," Marv said, "but I always get brown."

"Well, maybe you don't do it right."

"I know that already, and that's why I'm not going to mix any colors. How do you think it would look if we painted stripes?"

Ralph thought it would look great. Paul thought so too. They pried open the lids of the dozen or so cans of paint Marv brought out of the cellar. All of them had skins of dried paint across the top, and needed to be stirred and doctored up with doses of turpentine.

Marv started painting at one end of the trench with Daffodil Yellow. Paul at the other end selected Midnight Blue. Ralph working from the middle, straddled a stripe of Chinese Red. The finished work was dazzling. Even if Lucy had knocked over a can of American Beauty Rose while pointing out to Paul a spot he had missed, and Seymour had peppered the drying paint with clods of earth as he scrunched back and forth above, none of that was likely to show once the water was in. But once in, would it stay in? That was the final and most worrisome question. He would have to wait another agonizing day or so until the paint dried.

He put planks across the trench, and warned everybody to keep out. The next day, the paint was still tacky, so Marv and the crew put away tools, brushes and cans of paint. They swept the front stairs and walk. Seymour hosed down the sidewalk in front of the house, the garbage can and Lucy.

There were still a number of wet spots in the paint on the following day, and on the following day as well. Marv was up nearly the whole night before the day of Frances' return, worrying and planning. He decided to get up at dawn, and if the paint was dry, he'd put in the water before any of his loyal workers showed up. He'd get everything in order so that it would be ready before Frances arrived. He did not know what he would do if the paint was still wet. None of the various solutions he considered throughout the night seemed satisfactory, so very, very late, he decided that the paint *would* be dry, and the important thing was to get an early start.

He overslept. The crew was all ready and waiting for him. But the paint was dry. Everything was dry. The temperature was already 96°, and there wasn't a wet spot anywhere except in the sweat that poured off Marv and his workers as they lifted the boards from the top of the trench, and carried them out to the back.

Marv attached the garden hose to the water pipe in the basement. He carried it up the steps, and dropped the nozzle into the moat.

"Now?" shouted Ralph, from his post near the water pipe in the basement.

"Now!"

You could hear the water being turned on, the

hissing in the hose, a short silence, and then—the spluttering at the mouth, and you could see the water erupting out of the nozzle.

It took forever. The six of them stood there watching, joined after while by a growing band of spectators. Would it work or wouldn't it? The water seemed to be flowing endlessly from the mouth the hose yet nothing was happening inside the trench. What was the matter? What had he done wrong?

Marv lay down on the bridge, and leaned over the side. A puddle at the bottom of the moat began to take shape. It swelled and widened and rose. Marv reached down and touched it, and felt the birth of a stream under his fingers.

"Mama," Roslyn yelled, "I want to go swimming! Mama, can I go swimming?"

"No," said Roslyn's mother.

Roslyn took off her shoes.

"Did you hear what I said, Roslyn? I said no!"

Roslyn took off her socks.

"No is no!"

Roslyn jumped into the stream, and yelled, "Mama, can I?"

"I want to go too," said Stanford. He pulled off his shoes and socks and jumped in. He and Roslyn laughed and splashed and looked so cool that Seymour joined them too.

"I'm going to put on my bathing suit," Lucy cried, and ran off down the street.

The water reached the top of the trench, and Marv watched, hoping his calculations would prove correct. He had been careful to build up the wall on the street side of the stream higher than the inside wall. In this way, he planned for the overflow to irrigate the grassy plot where Frances' iris grew, even though at the present moment, the plot was far from grassy, and he was not sure exactly where the iris did grow.

Lucy returned in a bathing suit, and joined the swimmers. He had not thought of children swimming when he designed the stream, but why not? Some children swim in some streams. Why not this one? Marv watched the children swimming. He looked at the bright colors on the bottom of the stream, making the water appear a patchwork of reds, blues, greens, yellows, and every color in the world except brown. His eyes moved over the bridge to the bird bath, crowned with bells, up the front of the house to the weather vane whale, watchfully waiting in the hot, still day.

He hoped a wind would spring up before Frances came home. If he knew exactly when she was going to arrive, he would like to be hidden behind the living room window. He would like to see her face when she got out of the truck.

The crowd of onlookers continued to grow. "Marv!" somebody shouted. Stanford's mother was trying to elbow her way through the mass of people. He started toward her, and then, through the arms and legs and heads all around him, he heard the sound of a car parking.

"Frances," he shouted, "I'm coming, Frances."

He had to push and shove and beg to get through the crowd. She was standing there on the sidewalk, and somebody was handing her suitcase down to her, but she didn't see it. She was staring at the crowd.

"My God!" she cried when she saw him. "Marv, what happened? What's wrong?"

"Nothing, Frances," Marv said, laughing. How funny it was, her thinking something was wrong. He reached up and took her suitcase.

"Goodbye, Frances," a number of voices called as the truck began to drive off.

"Is Mama all right?" Frances cried.

"Everybody is all right, Frances," Marv said. "It's a surprise—for you. You just can't see it because of all the people, but come, I'll clear a path for you. And welcome home, Frances."

He took her hand, and pushed and pulled his way through the crowd. When they got to the bridge, Marv pointed to it, and asked, smiling, "Look at this, Frances. Do you know what it is?" Frances looked but she did not answer. "It's a bridge, Frances," Marv explained lovingly. "Look up, Frances." Obediently, Frances looked up. "It's a weather vane. Now, look there." Frances' eyes rested on the bird bath. "It's a bird bath. And now, Frances," Marv said slowly, enjoying every minute, "look *there!*"

But Frances' eyes had already found the stream, and the children bathing in its clear, brilliant waters.

"It's a stream. Like what you saw in Tibbetts Brook. Like what you said was so beautiful. Remember, Frances, you said you wished you could live in a place like that? Well, now you can. I made it for you, Frances—the stream, the bridge, the bird bath, and the weather vane. But, Frances, I want you to know that the bird bath revolves to scare off cats, and when the wind blows, the weather vane . . ."

Frances began to cry. She didn't say anything. She just began to cry. Then she ran up the stairs, and slammed the door behind her.

Marv looked at the bird bath, and he looked at the weather vane. He wrinkled his forehead, and he looked at the stream with all the children swimming in it. He tried to see it through Frances' eyes. How beautiful it all was! Even though she had cried, there could be no denying its beauty.

But why had she cried? Could it be that it was not useful? Like the lift he had made. That was not useful although it seemed very beautiful to him. Was it another failure then? Yes, it was. He had failed again, because he was unable to make anything useful, anything that would benefit anybody. That's why Frances had cried.

"Marvin!"

There was Stanford's mother again. Of course. Stanford had jumped into the stream with his clothes on. Mrs. Jackson was not likely to be enthusiastic about that. Wasn't there anything he could do right? He tried to collect his thoughts so he could apologize, but Mrs. Jackson reached out and took his arm. She was smiling.

"Marvin," she said, "you're worth your weight in gold."

"I'm sorry," Marv managed to say.

"I didn't know what I was going to do with Stanford this summer, and he's had the best summer he's ever had, thanks to you. And now a swimming pool! I had no idea what you were doing here, but how thoughtful of you to make a swimming pool for the little children. Look how happy they are. You're a wonderful boy, Marvin Green."

Then she kissed him, and handed him a nectarine from one of her packages. She asked him if he would mind watching Stanford while she put away her groceries, and to be sure to tell Stanford to come out if his lips turned blue.

Marv sat on the top step of the staircase, and bit into his nectarine. There certainly were a lot of people laughing down there. Nobody noticed him, and he ate greedily, wiping his mouth across the back of his hand when the nectarine spilled its juices all over his face.

Frances had cried. He had finally made something

that he *knew* was both beautiful and useful. But not to Frances. And why was that? Could he ever do anything that would please Frances? Shouldn't he, who admired her and accepted all her ideas, be able to do something she could admire and accept? It was complicated—too complicated for today. Another day, he would think it out, and try again.

He leaned back against the step, and thought dreamily about the two and a half remaining weeks before school started. He could do anything he liked now. Perhaps if the heat continued he might go to the pool with Ralph and Paul. He put both hands behind his neck, and stretched.

He was just opening his mouth to yawn when a picture, high and splendid, rose up in his mind. It happened so completely without warning that it turned the yawn into a hiccup. The real solution at long last! His beautiful, double ratchet handle, lying almost forgotten there in the garden. No, no, of course, not forgotten. He had been distracted, but now he knew what he really wanted to do in the time that was left to him before school started. Now he could follow through on the problem that had tantalized him for such a long, aching time.

He would build an escalator in the garden, and the double-ratchet handle would raise and lower it. He had nearly everything he needed—ropes, pulleys, planks and chains. A site? He needed a site. He stood up.

What about the southeast corner? There was nothing there that couldn't be moved or leveled. Yes, he believed that would be best, but he needn't be hasty. Thoughtfully, Marv moved through the crowd, down the basement steps, and out into his garden.

ABOUT THE AUTHOR

Marilyn Sachs, a native New Yorker, received her Bachelor of Arts degree from Hunter College and a Master's degree in Library Science from Columbia University. As a specialist in children's literature, she was with the Brooklyn Public Library for more than ten years and with the San Francisco Public Library for five years. Her familiarity with good books for children is evident in her own style and in the immediate success of her previous books. *Veronica Ganz* was selected by the American Library Association as one of the "Notable Children's Books of 1968."

Mrs. Sachs lives in San Francisco with her husband Morris, a sculptor; her son, Paul; and her daughter, Anne.

160